THE
MYSTERIOUS
WOODS
OF
WHISTLE
ROOT

THE
MYSTERIOUS
WOODS
OF
WHISTLE
ROOT

written by **Christopher Pennell**

illustrated by **Rebecca Bond**

HOUGHTON MIFFLIN HARCOURT

Boston   New York

For my wife and kids.   —C.P.

*For Thia, who is of course older than Carly,
but is a night child herself.   —R.B.*

Text copyright © 2013 by Christopher Pennell
Illustrations copyright © 2013 by Rebecca Bond

www.hmhbooks.com

Text set in Arno Pro

Library of Congress Cataloging-in-Publication Data
Pennell, Christopher.
The mysterious woods of Whistle Root /
by Christopher Pennell ; [illustrations, Rebecca Bond].
p. cm.
Summary: Eleven-year-old Carly Bean Bitters, an orphan, can only sleep during
the day and feels very lonely until she meets a rat, Lewis, and sets off on an
adventure to figure out what is threatening the woods and its inhabitants.
ISBN 978-0-547-79263-7
[1. Adventure and adventurers — Fiction. 2. Rats — Fiction. 3. Owls — Fiction.
4. Forests and forestry — Fiction. 5. Musicians — Fiction. 6. Monsters —
Fiction. 7. Orphans — Fiction.] I. Bond, Rebecca, 1972– ill. II. Title.
PZ7.P384628Mys 2013
[Fic] — dc23
2012039968

Manufactured in the United States of America
DOC 10 9 8 7 6 5 4 3 2 1
4500427520

CONTENTS

CHAPTER ONE

THE DANCING OWLS

I n a small town called Whistle Root, rats play music in the moonlight. They play on the very rooftops there. You can hear them if you listen closely in the middle of the night when there's a slight breeze blowing. Who knows why they like breezes, but they do. And moonlight. You'll never hear a rat playing music without moonlight.

The music can be scary. It sounds as if someone left a radio playing in the closet. But if you're brave enough to look in the closet, you won't find anything. And if you're even braver and look out your window, the music will stop completely.

All of which leads me to the story of a girl named Carly who looked out the window of her upstairs room one night and saw a squash sitting on the roof.

NOW, VEGETABLES HAD BEEN APPEARING on roofs all over Whistle Root for several weeks that summer. So when Carly looked out her window and saw the squash sitting there, it wasn't a complete surprise.

Still, it's odd seeing vegetables on the roof. We expect to see them in the garden or on our dinner plates. We don't expect to look out our windows and see them staring back at us.

But Carly felt more curious than scared. She opened her window and waited to see if anything else would appear. She waited for the music to start again too, which had caused her to look out the window in the first place.

But there was just the moonlight and the squash and a slight breeze blowing.

"I notice that you have a squash on your roof, dear," said one of her older neighbors, walking by late one evening. "How lovely. I only have broccoli."

CARLY'S FULL NAME WAS CARLY Bean Bitters. Her parents had named her partly after a great-great-grandmother named Magritta Bean, whom everybody had just called Gritty. Carly had to be thankful that she hadn't ended up being named Gritty Bitters.

Carly was small for her age, which was eleven years old. Her hair was dark and her skin was pale. Strangely, she had never been able to sleep at night. She could only sleep during the day. It was a troublesome affliction, a contrary clock, and there was nothing she could do to change it.

"She hasn't got an ailment . . . she's just an oddity," Carly had overheard her doctor say once, after none of the pills he had prescribed to make her sleep at night had worked.

Every night Carly stayed in her room, drinking hot tea and sitting in her chair by the little brick fireplace she felt so lucky to have. She read books, waiting for

Every night Carly stayed in her room.

the sun to rise so that she could finally go to sleep and leave the lonely, wakeful hours behind.

She also dreamed of a life in the sunlight, outside of her little room that too often felt like a prison, despite its coziness.

But that was asking too much, she knew.

She would settle for a friend.

CARLY WATCHED THE ROOF EVERY night from her window; she wanted to see if whatever had left the squash would come back. But several days passed and the squash began to rot and attract flies. Birds picked at it and took pieces away to eat. And then the rain came and washed what was left of it off the roof.

Eventually, Carly stopped watching from her window.

But moonlight and summer breezes always return. And one day, there was a brand-new squash sitting in the exact same spot as the one that had recently rotted.

That night, Carly kept her window open and sat in a chair beside it, watching the roof again. She was startled when she heard someone ask, "Excuse me, can you play the horn?"

There on the windowsill was a rat
holding a fiddle and a little red horn.

"You see, I can't perform with
just the squash," said the rat.
"And it would be a great embarrassment to have two vegetables in the band. I really
shouldn't ask you but the owls took poor Fenny last
night."

Carly didn't know what to say, since she hadn't
understood what the rat was talking about. "Are you
the one who put the squash on the roof?" she finally
asked.

"Of course," said the rat. "Fenny and I had to have
someone to play the drum."

"The squash plays the drum?" asked Carly.

"No, not really," the rat replied with a sigh.

A breeze came in through the open window and
moved the curtains gently. The light from a full moon
cast a blue glow over Carly's room.

"It's such a good night for music," said the rat. "We
really shouldn't waste it."

"MY NAME'S LEWIS," THE RAT told Carly, and handed the little red horn to her. "And this is Fenny's horn. You'll have to learn to play it, of course, but mainly you just blow into it and think sad or happy thoughts."

They were standing on the roof and Carly held the horn, which was about as big as her little finger.

"How did you get the squash onto the roof?" she asked. "It's bigger than you are."

"It's a simple matter of breezes," explained Lewis. "We ride the breezes to the rooftops. And a breeze is certainly strong enough to carry a squash. Now remember, sad songs are slower than happy songs." And with that advice, he began to play a sad song on his fiddle that made Carly think of the moon. She blew into the little red horn and thought sad thoughts and made sad music too. As she played she watched the moon, which was just above the treetops. She was frightened when she saw shadows fly across its face.

"What were those?" she asked.

Lewis stopped playing.

"It's the owls," he said. "But it doesn't look like they're heading for our rooftop. We should be safe tonight."

"Why did they take your friend Fenny?"

"To eat him, I suppose. And before that they took Walter. That's why Fenny and I had to bring the squash here. A band has to have three members, you know. No more and no less. One for the fiddle, one for the horn, and one for the drum."

"But the squash can't play the drum," said Carly.

"Oh, I know that," said Lewis. "But he could always learn to play, couldn't he? If he would just practice, I mean. He has at least a week before he begins to rot."

SEVERAL NIGHTS PASSED AND LEWIS visited Carly on each one. He was a wonderful fiddler, and Carly loved listening to his music and learning to play the horn along with him. After so many years of sitting alone in her room, it felt as if a new world had appeared, right outside her window.

But it was a world of danger, too.

"That horn is very old," Lewis said on the fourth night. "*Please* be careful with it."

Carly picked up the little red horn. She had been startled by shadows flying near the house and had dropped it on the roof. "Why don't we play in my room?" she asked as she looked around nervously. "We'd be much safer there."

Lewis looked at Carly as if she had said something ridiculous. "We always play outside in the moonlight."

"Well, maybe we could play on the ground then. There are more places to hide from the owls down there."

"We always play up high," said Lewis.

"But that doesn't make sense!" said Carly. "Why do you make it so easy for the owls to get you?"

Lewis plucked the strings of his fiddle and stared at the empty roof next to theirs. "The owls never bothered us before," he finally said. "I should think they'll start dancing again soon."

"Dancing?" said Carly in surprise.

"Well, it's more like they hop from foot to foot and flap their wings. But I don't know what you'd call it if not dancing."

"They used to dance when you played music?"

"Of course. They would listen from the trees and dance on the branches. It's always been that way and I'm sure it will be that way again. But they won't start dancing if we don't play any music. Shall we play another song?"

Carly sighed. She had learned that there was little point talking to Lewis when he was ready to play music. They were about to begin when a large shadow flew over them and headed toward the trees just outside Carly's yard. While they watched, it turned and flew back toward them, slowly at first but then with increasing speed.

"Keep playing!" yelled Lewis as he began to fiddle faster.

But Carly was too scared to play the little horn. She turned to jump back through her window. As she did, something sharp grabbed her shoulders and lifted her off the rooftop.

CHAPTER TWO

BREEZA MEEZY

hen Carly opened her eyes, she was floating on her back in a pond. She could see the dark sky and bright stars above her.

She didn't remember fainting, but she knew she must have, because she didn't remember anything between being lifted off the rooftop and waking up in the pond.

She felt calm, and perhaps that was because the water was warm and comforting. Her ears were underwater too, which made everything peaceful and quiet.

A breeze began to blow, and Lewis came flying out of the night with his fiddle and the little red horn. He landed gently on Carly's stomach.

"We should get out of the water and start walking,"

he said. "If we get back before daylight, we might have time to play a few more songs."

When they were out of the pond and walking home through the woods, Carly put the little red horn in a pocket on the front of her wet nightgown. She noticed that Lewis was tapping trees with his fiddle bow every now and then.

"Why are you doing that?" she asked.

"To make sure we're not dreaming."

Carly waited a few moments but Lewis did not explain further. "I don't understand," she said.

Lewis stopped walking and looked up at her. "If the tree trunks shimmer when you tap them, it means you're dreaming."

"If they shimmer? Like how?"

"Like the surface of a pond when you drop a pebble in it," said Lewis. "Shimmer trees exist only in dreams, you see. At least that's what the old rats say."

He started walking again and Carly followed. "I guess you were too heavy for that owl. He kept flying lower and lower until your feet were dragging in the water and then he just dropped you in. I bet he had never tried to carry a child before — even one as small as you."

A breeze began to blow and Carly felt a chill go through her. She had always watched the woods from her window at night but had never gone into them.

"Could you play something on your fiddle?" Carly asked. She thought Lewis's music would make their walk through the dark woods less scary.

"Of course not," he said. "A band has to have three members. One for the fiddle, one for the horn, and one for the drum."

"You can't play a song by yourself?"

Lewis didn't respond at first. "I never thought to try," he finally said, and stopped walking. He cautiously put his fiddle under his chin and raised his bow to the strings. He played a few notes and then stopped and looked around as if waiting for something to happen. When nothing did, he played a few more. And when he finally realized that playing by himself was something he could really do, he relaxed, and began

Lewis continued to play as they made their way home.

walking again, continuing to play as they made their way home.

After Lewis had played several songs, Carly took the little red horn out of her pocket and lifted it to her lips like a small flute. She could already play it quite well. She had inherited a talent for music from her father.

Anyone who heard them as they walked through the woods that night would have thought a small parade was passing by.

CARLY'S FATHER WAS A TRAVELING musician who had died when a tornado struck the theater where he was performing. Her mother had died two years later after a sudden illness. The main thing Carly remembered about her father was his music, which had been beautiful. The main thing she remembered about her mother was her gentleness and how hard she had tried to stay awake every night to be with Carly, even when she could barely keep her own eyes open. Even after she got sick. She had wanted to protect her dearly loved daughter, her night child, from loneliness.

An orphan at five years old, Carly had been sent to live with her aunt, her mother's much older sister, because there weren't any other living relatives. The aunt was a grim woman who provided Carly with food and a room, but not much else. And she never stayed up with her. She was too tired from the long hours she spent working in the town's rundown doll factory, painting face after face on an endless procession of round little heads. She fell asleep every day almost as soon as she got home.

In many ways, it was as if Carly had been living alone for the past six years.

But really, she wasn't alone anymore. She saw Lewis every night. And on the night after the owl dropped her in the pond, Lewis asked her to meet him in the woods.

Carly had agreed — it seemed safer than playing music on her roof — and she was now trying to follow the directions he'd given her. He'd told her to walk along the creek behind her house until she came to the old whistle root tree. The problem was that there were lots of whistle root trees along the creek, and they were *all* old, and Carly didn't know which one Lewis had been talking about.

In fact, there weren't any young whistle root trees. At least, no one in the town of Whistle Root had ever seen one. And if anybody would have seen them, it would have been the townspeople, because the trees didn't grow anywhere else. The whistle root trees were so unique that the town had been named after them.

What made whistle root trees unique? Their whistle roots — little hollow roots about the size of fingers that stuck up out of the ground and had an opening in the tip to collect rain. You could snap a whistle root off at its base and blow through the raindrop-collecting end, and make a whistle so loud that your ears would ring for several minutes afterward.

And the whistle root leaves weren't flat like the leaves of other trees. They hung down from the branches like upside-down ice cream cones, hollow on the inside and pointy on top. They were dark and green and when breezes blew, they swung back and forth like a million little bells ringing silently.

There were younger trees like oaks, sweetgums, and hackberries, but the whistle root trees were the old giants and they dominated the woods.

Carly stood by the tallest whistle root tree with the thickest trunk she could find, thinking it had to be one of the oldest. She called Lewis's name several times into the darkness. There was no answer. She

turned slowly in a circle and searched
the woods with her flashlight, but saw
only trees and the creek and shadows.

An owl hooted nearby and Carly suddenly wanted
to run home to the safety of her room. But the thought
of her empty chair waiting for her made her feel so sad
that she stopped, bent down and snapped off a whistle root, and began to blow instead.

She let the whistle rise until it was very loud. It had
been so quiet that the whistle root's whistle sounded
like a siren warning the woods of danger. The sound

seemed to move in all
directions, and echoed through the trees after she
had stopped blowing.

Carly waited to see what would happen. Soon she
heard a familiar voice floating through the air say, "I
thought that had to be you."

Lewis landed and led her along the creek until it
took a bend to the left. There, the bank rose ten feet or
so straight up in a wall of rock. And on a small patch

of ground between the creek and the rock wall stood the oldest-looking whistle root tree that Carly had ever seen.

"Well, aren't you coming?" she heard Lewis say. She realized he wasn't beside her anymore. His voice sounded as if it was coming from across the creek. She searched with her flashlight and found him peeking out from behind the old whistle root tree. "The creek's narrow here," he said. "You can hop across it."

Carly hesitated for a moment, but then hopped over the creek and followed Lewis into the narrow space between the tree and the rock wall behind it. There was an opening there, in the wall, that she hadn't been able to see before. It was much taller than a rat would need. In fact, Carly was able to walk right in without bending over at all. And after she had passed through, she found something surprising indeed.

Spread out before her was a village of little houses. They covered the floor of the large cave and their windows were lit up like lanterns. She saw a blue house with windows shaped like the moon and stars and a white one with windows carved in the shape of different birds. Each house in the village looked completely unique. And behind the houses, toward the back of the cave, was what appeared to be a small tower. Everything glowed quietly with the flickering firelight coming from the little windows. Carly had never seen anything so wondrous and magical in her entire life.

"This way," said Lewis as he led her through the village, heading toward the tower. "Breeza Meezy wants to see you right away."

"Who wants to see me?" asked Carly, but Lewis didn't answer. She could see rats coming to the doors and windows of the houses now. Their eyes were wide with interest and surprise. They began to leave their houses and followed Carly and Lewis as they walked.

When they reached the tower, Carly saw an old wooden chair beside it. Not a chair for a rat, but a chair for a person. Carly wondered if she was supposed to sit in it. She was about to ask Lewis when an elegant female voice began to speak.

"Good evening," said the voice. "It is an honor to have you here. I am the Breeza of this village. I am Breeza Meezy."

Carly saw a white rat standing on the top of the tower.

"Please, have a seat," said Breeza Meezy. "I apologize

Spread out before her was a village of little houses.

that there are so few of us to greet you, but the owls have taken most of our musicians, as I believe you know."

Carly nodded and sat down in the chair. The other rats gathered around.

"I must say," continued Breeza Meezy. "When I first heard that one of our musicians had asked a child to play the horn, I was very angry. There are strict rules regarding these matters." She looked down at Lewis, who was standing at the foot of Carly's chair, with disapproval in her eyes. "For as we all know, when a musician dies, a vegetable takes his place until a suitable replacement is found and trained. There are no exceptions to this rule."

Carly noticed that Breeza Meezy appeared to be very old. Aside from being white, she also moved more slowly than the other rats. And her eyes were slightly clouded, as if someone had squeezed a tiny drop of milk into them.

"I have learned that young Lewis has broken other rules as well," said Breeza Meezy. "He played his fiddle without a horn or a drum to accompany him, and he played music while on the ground." There was whispering among the crowd of rats. Lewis stared at his feet. The whispers grew louder until Breeza Meezy silenced them with a wave of her hand. "It is our duty as rats to play music," she said. "But it is our duty, as well, to follow the rules. And as Breeza, it is my duty to punish those who disobey them . . ."

There was a terrible pause, and Carly worried that something bad was going to happen to Lewis. She was about to say something in his defense when Breeza Meezy began to speak again.

"However," she said, somewhat more kindly now. "Perhaps I will forgive his disobedience. He has brought me a child, who may be of some help to us. There is an old saying among us rats: 'A white cradle in the woods brings hope.' I would like to place a white cradle in the woods as soon as possible. Will you assist me with this?"

CHAPTER THREE

THE WHITE CRADLE

arly lived in a large old falling-down house on the edge of the woods of Whistle Root. Repairs were never made. Her aunt didn't have money for that. When pieces fell off, like shingles, shutters, and chimney bricks, they lay in the tall grass untouched, as if the hope was they would recover on their own and then climb dutifully back into place.

The night after visiting the rats' cave, Carly searched the house's dark attic, looking for a cradle.

She had of course agreed to help Breeza Meezy. It seemed certain that Lewis would escape punishment if she did. But placing a white cradle in the woods was more difficult than she had planned. She discovered that there wasn't a cradle in her aunt's house. Why would there be after all? Her aunt didn't have any children. Carly also had no money with which to buy a

Repairs were never made. There wasn't money for that.

cradle. And because she slept during the day, she had never been able to make friends; therefore, she couldn't look in their houses or ask them for money.

But Lewis found a cradle in a neighbor's garage. It was covered in cobwebs and obviously hadn't been used in a very long time. They took it from the garage late one night, painted it white, and placed it in the woods near the rats' cave as Breeza Meezy had instructed them to do. Carly silently promised to return the cradle when the rats no longer needed it.

It was windy that night, and the empty cradle looked spooky sitting in the darkness among the moving trees.

"What happens now?" Carly asked Lewis. He looked at the

cradle and at the trees all around them. He tapped one of the trees with his fiddle bow and it didn't shimmer. "I should tell Breeza Meezy," he said, and walked in the direction of the cave.

Carly began to follow him. But when she turned to take one last look at the cradle, she was surprised to see that there was now something inside it.

In the middle of the cradle, a red marching band hat had appeared — one of those tall, fuzzy ones with a little black brim and a strap to attach it under the chin. It was smaller than they normally are and looked as if it had been made for a doll with a head the size of an apple.

She turned to look for Lewis but he was already gone.

The wind was getting stronger and Carly's dark hair was blowing wildly about.

The hat looked harmless. She picked it up and felt how soft it was. Then she turned it over, and that is when she saw the note.

A small white card on the inside said:

BEWARE OF BROKEN ROCKS!

I wonder what that means, Carly thought.

It was a note in a hat in a cradle in the woods. Carly decided that it was time to go home.

BACK AT HER HOUSE IN the dark kitchen, Carly found a cold pot that held half an inch of watery brown stew — the remains of her aunt's dinner and the only food in the house. Starving, she finished it in four meager spoonfuls.

She climbed the stairs and fell asleep in her bed as the sun rose. A favorite tune that Lewis often played flittered through her dreams while her aunt's alarm clock clattered in a distant part of the house.

The next night as soon as he landed on her roof, Carly told Lewis about the hat. She also told him what the note had said.

Lewis stared at her for a moment, as if patiently listening to her describe some crazy dream she'd had. Then he made a little joke about that being the kind of useless advice he'd expect from a hat, and lifted his fiddle to his chin to play.

But before his bow even touched the strings, an owl swooped in, barely missed him, and grabbed the squash and the drum instead.

"Lewis!" yelled Carly, as she watched him jump from the roof and fly after the disappearing owl. She quickly climbed down the young oak tree that stood beside her house and ran straight into the woods after him.

She knew Lewis was trying to get the drum back. He had told her before that each instrument was very old and that the rats didn't know who had made them or how to make any more.

She ran as fast as she could, desperate to protect Lewis, and was soon out of the trees and crossing a small field. But her feet struck something hard and she cried out in surprise and fell to the ground. She was scrambling to get up and start running again when Lewis came walking toward her.

"The breeze died and dropped me in a bush," he said unhappily.

Carly looked around nervously but didn't see any more owls.

She wondered what she'd tripped over and turned back to where she'd fallen. And there, she found something that made her raise her hand to her mouth in surprise.

It was a broken rock.

Actually, it was half of a broken rock. She looked around and found the other half and saw that they fit together, with a hollow inside, almost like an egg. *Beware of broken rocks,* the message in the little red hat had said. What did it all mean?

Most of all, Carly wondered, what had been inside the hollow rock?

CHAPTER FOUR

The Rising Creek

he next night, Carly walked to the rats' cave alone. She followed the creek as she had done before and moved quickly through the woods, hoping not to encounter any owls.

It was breezy but the moon wasn't out, so she knew Lewis wouldn't come to her rooftop. She didn't understand why the rats played music only in moonlight, although that wasn't nearly so odd as their other rules. The vegetables replacing lost musicians made no sense to her at all.

Carly intended to tell Breeza Meezy about the marching band hat and the note that had appeared in the cradle. She also wanted to talk with her about the broken rock.

"Always heed the wisdom of hats," Lewis had quipped when she'd tried to discuss it with him. "If you had, I'm sure you would have seen the rock—in the dark—on the ground—while running—and not fallen over it."

Carly worried that the hat was trying to warn them of more than a tripping hazard. But warn them of what? The broken rock resembled a recently hatched egg. What could hatch from a rock?

Carly had almost reached the cave when there was a sudden rush of chattering noises, as if someone had poured out a barrelful of lost teeth. She spun toward the sound, shining her flashlight on the creek. Did the water seem higher than before?

As she watched, the creek rose quickly, flooding the streambed and tumbling off downstream in the direction she'd been going. She had to scramble to higher ground to avoid getting swept away by the unexpected torrent.

Swept away! The rats' village! Carly ran the short distance that remained to the cave. She saw the old whistle root tree, but there was no way to reach it — she was on the wrong side of the creek. The water had already climbed several feet up the tree's trunk and was rushing into the cave behind it.

"Lewis!" she yelled. "Breeza Meezy!"

Why didn't they fly out? The night was full of breezes. Surely some of them were entering the cave.

Not knowing what else to do, Carly pulled out the little red horn she'd brought and blew into it violently, making a horrible squall. Was she too late to warn them?

To her relief, small dark shapes soon began flying out of the cave and over the creek.

"Not your best music," said Lewis, when he landed on the ground beside her. He was drenched but holding his fiddle.

The other rats landed around her too. They looked wet, frightened, and bewildered by the creek's sudden anger.

"QUICK!" YELLED BREEZA MEEZY. "FLY through the woods! Every rat in a different direction!"

She had not finished saying these words when owls began to swoop down on them. They caught the rats who weren't able to get off the ground quick enough and chased the others through the air.

Carly grabbed a large stick and swung at the dark shapes of the owls as they flew around her. She frantically looked for Lewis, but didn't see him. She was about to call his name when an owl seized her hair in its talons. She felt terrible pain as it tried to lift her, but she smacked it with her stick. The startled owl screeched, released her hair, and flapped its wings mightily to get away.

Other owls began to scratch her arms with their talons as they flew past. They were flying so close that she felt their feathers brush her skin. The stick was yanked from her hand and she felt as if flapping wings were all around her. She was having trouble breathing.

Carly grabbed a large stick and swung.

And she stopped breathing entirely when she heard the whistle.

It was so loud that she covered her ears with her hands and still couldn't block its sound. Pain caused her to squeeze her eyes shut and double over as if she was ill. It felt as if someone was piercing her head with a pencil, into one ear and out the other. The sound was louder than anything she had ever heard before. It blasted and blared, tearing through the night four or five times, and then everything became silent.

After a moment, Carly looked up. The owls were gone. Beside her on the ground stood five rats, each one holding a whistle root. So they had made the terrible-sounding whistle? How loud it had been!

Other rats drifted down from the trees, and Carly was relieved to see Lewis and Breeza Meezy among them. The flooded creek subsided and the rats were soon able to go back in the cave. It was too dangerous to stay outside; the owls could return at any time.

The houses were damaged but they were still there, and the rats gathered dry wood and lit fires to dry the cave out.

Lewis climbed onto his roof and just sat there holding his fiddle. The roof was sagging dangerously, but he didn't seem to notice. Almost all the musicians were gone now; the thought of playing with vegetables for the rest of his life couldn't have pleased him.

Carly found the chair she had used on her previous visit and moved it back to its spot beside the tower. She hadn't noticed before, but the chair had a beautiful carving of a crescent moon on it. She traced its outline with her finger.

Most of the rats were inside their houses, busy with repairs and figuring out what and who had been lost. Carly couldn't resist getting down on her hands and knees and peeking through the windows to see what was going on inside. If a rat noticed her, she would smile and ask if they needed any help. "No, thank you, dear," was the polite reply she heard again and again.

She crawled through the village and soon found herself back at the tower, which was ablaze with light from its many fireplaces. Breeza Meezy was there, watching the village. She looked at Carly and gestured toward the chair. Carly pulled herself up and sat down.

"Thank you for your help tonight," said Breeza Meezy. "The water put out our fires so quickly, and we couldn't see anything in the darkness. There was so much confusion — we couldn't find the way out of the cave. But the sound of your horn guided us. All of us would have drowned or been taken by the owls if you hadn't come."

"It was those rats who saved you," said Carly. "The ones who blew the whistle roots. How did they know to do that?"

"It's an old trick we use when other animals try to

enter the cave. But we've never used it against the owls before . . . until tonight."

"Why not?" asked Carly.

Breeza Meezy stared off toward the entrance to the cave. "We've known these owls all of our lives," she said sadly. "Many of them are old enough to have watched my grandfather play, when he was our finest fiddler. And most have danced to Lewis's music since his first night on a roof. Do you know how sensitive an owl's ears are? They can hear beetles burrowing underground and the flutterings of a dragonfly's heart. They're our friends, regardless of the current attacks. We haven't wanted to hurt them . . ."

Carly didn't understand. The owls might once have been the rats' friends, but now?

She felt the carving of the crescent moon against her back and asked Breeza Meezy where the chair had come from.

"My grandmother told me it belonged to the Moon King," she said. "But she didn't know who he was. He lived in these woods a long time ago, and I'm afraid his story has been forgotten."

Then Carly told Breeza Meezy about the message in the cradle and the broken rock she had found. Breeza Meezy was very interested, but didn't know what it could mean. Their conversation was interrupted by the sound of another whistle coming from the front of the cave.

A rat standing guard had seen another owl and had blown his whistle root to alert the village, although there really wasn't any danger. The space behind the old whistle root tree in front of the cave was too narrow for the owls with wings outstretched to fly through.

Carly suddenly realized that it was almost morning. And she remembered with a shock that summer was over and today was the first day of school. She quickly said goodbye to Breeza Meezy, promised to come back the next night, and ran home through the woods as fast as she could.

CHAPTER FIVE

THE ENDROOT

ummer was Carly's favorite season because she could sleep all day. The end of summer meant school. And once school started, she would hear the same seven words over and over again: *Carly Bean Bitters, you must wake up!* She would hear them at home from her aunt and at school from her teachers.

She had begged her aunt in the past to let her stay home and study on her own at night, but her aunt had always refused. "You'll be normal in this, at least!" she had said.

And so, Carly's sixth year of school began as all the others had. She had barely gotten to her desk when her eyes began to close and she promptly fell asleep.

Her new teacher, Ms. Hankel, had been warned about her no doubt. She shook Carly roughly to wake her and then walked away without saying a word.

Carly found that her desk was slightly apart from the others and directly under an air-conditioning vent that blew a constant stream of cold air at her. Luckily, she had worn long sleeves, even though it was warm outside, to hide the scratches the owls had made.

She also noticed that hers was the only desk with a floor lamp beside it, with what appeared to be an especially large and bright bulb.

She suffered sleepily through the morning and finally found her self in the library for a short study period. She immediately be-gan looking for books about the history of Whistle Root. What Breeza Meezy had said about the Moon King intrigued her, and she wanted to see if she could find out anything about him.

"You should try this one," a voice said.

Based on the size of the chair in the rats' cave, Carly could tell that the Moon King had been a person and not a rat. But who was he? Had he played music with the rats as she did? Why was he called the Moon King?

Carly could find only one short book about Whistle Root, but it didn't say anything about the Moon King, and the disappointment must have been clear on her face.

"You should try this one," a voice said.

Carly looked up and saw Green Pitcher, a boy from her class. He was skinny and tall, and wore glasses. And despite his name, he had bright red hair. He was holding out a book to her.

Carly was surprised. Normally the other kids didn't talk to her. They thought she was strange, falling asleep all the time and living in that scary old house by the woods. But Carly thanked Green and took the book and sat down at a table. The book was very old and she looked through it quickly but still didn't find anything.

"You should try the secret pages," said Green, and Carly realized that he had joined her. He turned to the middle of the book and lifted out several pieces of folded brownish paper. He handed them to Carly.

The papers were very old and thin and crinkled when she touched them. She unfolded them carefully and saw writing, and this is what she read:

The STORY of the WHISTLE ROOT TREES

There once was a land called the Endroot where nothing would grow. No seed would sprout if you planted it. The roots of plants and trees would come to its edge and turn back as if frightened. It was literally where roots ended.

The ground was made of ashes. And the wind would blow the ashes into terrifying storms that filled the air and blocked the sun. It was always dark and cold there.

No animals or people lived in the Endroot. There was, however, one family that traveled there frequently. They were musicians, and they performed for whoever would pay them in the five kingdoms that surrounded the Endroot.

One day, when the air wasn't as thick with ash as usual, and you could even see the sun, a giant bird appeared in the sky. It was carrying a woman, and it dropped her into the Endroot and flew back in the direction from which it had come.

This wasn't as surprising as you might think. It was a common punishment in all five of the surrounding kingdoms to drop criminals into the Endroot and hope they would travel to one of the other kingdoms, if they survived at all. The traveling family of musicians avoided these people because you never knew if they were dangerous. They also had little food or water to share with strangers.

However, when the family reached the woman, she did not seem dangerous. She sat on the ground and watched them with her amber eyes but did not speak. Her hair and skin were quickly turning gray with ash. A man from the family walked over to her and asked what her crime had been. He was curious. They didn't often see women punished this way.

"I offered them a bag of seeds," the woman said.

The man laughed. "I'm sure your crime
was greater than that," he said, and walked on,
expecting nothing but more lies if he asked any
more questions.

A young boy from the family, who had heard
their conversation, snuck away and made his
way back to the woman. "Did you really only
offer them a bag of seeds?"

The woman nodded.

"Were they poisonous?"

The woman shook her head. "They were
only seeds," she said, and smiled. She could tell
that the boy had a good heart, so she offered
him a further explanation. "They thought
I was a witch," she said. "That's why they
dropped me here. It's funny how people will
punish you for the slightest little thing."

The boy, who had seen his own family
punished simply for being poor, could certainly
sympathize with that. And as the woman
seemed kind, he told her he would bring
her what food and water he could until they
reached the next kingdom. "Follow our tracks,"

he told her. "But stay far enough behind that the others can't see you."

The boy took care of the woman as he had promised, and she survived her long walk through the Endroot. On the last day of their journey, she gave him a gift. She pulled a small bag from a pocket in her dress and placed it in his hand. "Take these seeds," she said. "And whenever you travel in the Endroot, plant them in the ashes. Plant them everywhere, and one day you will have a kingdom of your own."

It was an odd request. But as the years passed and the boy and his family traveled through the Endroot, he planted the seeds as the woman had instructed him to do. He knew it was foolish and that the seeds would never grow, but he planted them with great care anyway.

And to the boy's great surprise, the seeds did grow. They grew into trees of all sorts and sizes. Trees that he had never seen before and could not have imagined. His favorites, however, were the ones with the musical roots and the leaves that reminded him of bells. He began to

call them whistle root trees
and was especially happy
when a new one sprouted.

AS SOON AS CARLY HAD fin-
ished reading, she searched the
book for more hidden pages. But
the bell rang and Green said he
had to hide it before going back
to class. "I don't want anyone else
to find it," he explained. But he
promised to show it to her again
and Carly agreed to meet him at
the same table the next day.

"Do you think the story's true?"
she asked him.

"Maybe," he said.

"Why did you show it to me?"

Green shrugged, refolded the
papers very carefully, and placed
them in the book. Then he looked around
as if to make sure no one was following him,
grabbed the book, and disappeared down a
dark aisle in the back of the library.

Carly couldn't resist following him. But when she looked down the aisle, she didn't see him anywhere.

That's odd, she thought. Without time to investigate further, she gathered up her things and trudged back to her cold and brightly lit desk.

CARLY WENT TO THE CAVE that night. She helped the rats with their repairs and, in the firelight, told them the story of the Endroot and the whistle root trees. None of them had heard of the Endroot before, not even Breeza Meezy.

"We've lost so many stories," was all that she could say.

THE NEXT DAY AT SCHOOL, Green wasn't in class. Still, during the study period, Carly waited for him at the same table in the library just in case — but he never showed up.

When the bell rang, and Carly got up to go back to her desk, a girl from her class named Hetta stuck out her foot and tripped her. Carly fell to the floor on her face.

"Look! She's fallen asleep again!" said Hetta, and everybody laughed.

In the afternoon Carly really did fall asleep, and Ms. Hankel knelt by her desk and blew a whistle loudly in her ear. Carly woke up swinging her arms wildly and struck Ms. Hankel hard. She had imagined that the owls were attacking her again.

She went to the principal's office and explained that it had been an accident. She didn't tell him that she had thought owls were attacking her; she figured he probably thought she was weird enough as it was.

She was finally allowed to go back to her classroom, where she apologized to Ms. Hankel.

"Very well," said Ms. Hankel curtly, not looking at Carly and pretending to be busy examining a paper clip.

Back at her desk, Carly looked out the window and saw smoke rising from somewhere deep within the woods. She panicked for a moment, thinking that the woods were on fire.

But as she watched, the smoked stayed the same and didn't seem to be spreading.

Did someone live out there?

Before she could think about it more, a blast of cold air hit her and she saw that Ms. Hankel was adjusting the thermostat.

"Bit hot in here," she said, smiling unpleasantly.

Carly saw a bruise forming around Ms. Hankel's right eye and realized that her school year had gotten off to a very bad start indeed.

CHAPTER SIX

SMOKE AND WHISPERS

hat night, Carly and Lewis walked through the woods trying to find the source of the smoke she had seen from school. Lewis wasn't happy about this. The moon was out and he wanted to play music.

"I already put a new squash on your roof," he complained.

Carly had insisted that they go. She hadn't been able to stop thinking about the Moon King, even though Breeza Meezy had said he'd lived a long time ago. Could he still be out there? And if he was, could he help the rats? She grew heartsick at the thought of the owls taking Lewis from her, which seemed more likely with each passing night. He was so reckless when he played his fiddle.

Carly also had another reason for seeking the Moon

King. Something inside her clutched desperately to the notion that he might have answers — answers to questions she had been asking her entire life, such as why was she awake every night? Why was she different? Her parents hadn't known and her aunt definitely didn't. Was there anyone else in the world like her? Or was she just an oddity, as the doctor had said?

She knew it was nothing but foolish hope (like wishing on stars and dandelions), but could the Moon King know things that no one else did? And if he didn't, would anyone?

Carly and Lewis stopped at the white cradle. Carly had promised Breeza Meezy she would let her know if anything else strange appeared in it. The red hat was still there, and Carly was surprised to see a new note inside. She read it aloud. It said:

Beware of whispers!

"What does that mean?" she asked Lewis.

"Probably that we should talk louder," he said, and set off through the woods again.

Carly shook her head, put the note in her pocket, and followed him. She hadn't forgotten the previous note or the broken rock it had predicted. But what danger was there in *whispers?*

As they walked, Lewis kept hopping onto breezes and flying above the trees so he could see the smoke and make sure they were going in the right direction.

"Why don't I just fly ahead?" he said. "I'll be there and back in no time."

"You can't blow enough whistle roots to protect yourself," said Carly. She had five whistle roots in her pocket and planned to use them if the owls attacked again. She had tied them together like a pan flute.

"But what if the clouds cover the moon?" asked Lewis. "Without its light, I won't be able to see the smoke."

Carly asked if he saw any clouds while flying above the trees and Lewis reluctantly admitted that he did not.

"This is taking forever," he complained. "You're too slow." And then he stopped, struck by an idea, and said, "Maybe I could teach you to fly."

"You could?" Carly was amazed at the suggestion.

"Sure," said Lewis. "It's easy. Put your foot in the air, wait for a breeze, and then see if you can find the tisks with your toes."

"What's a tisk?"

Lewis stared at her.

"What?" asked Carly. "I've never heard of them before."

Lewis's little shoulders seemed to slump.

"Oh, just tell me, for Pete's sake," said Carly. "You're wasting time." Lewis could be so difficult, but that often made Carly feel as if they had been friends for ages. And since she had never had a friend, the comfortable bickering made her feel good.

Lewis took a deep breath. "Okay," he finally said. "Put your foot in the air and tell me what a breeze feels like."

Carly did as he said and felt the breeze flowing across the bottom of her bare foot.

It was hard to describe what it felt like. It felt like a

breeze. It was slightly cool and made her foot tingle and gave her a slight shiver. But that was how the breeze made her feel. It was not how the breeze itself felt.

"Smooth," she finally said, unable to describe it any other way.

"Ah, but it's not," said Lewis. "It may feel smooth at first, but if you really pay attention, you'll find that it has little bumps and dents. Those are the tisks." He put his own toes in the air. "There's a tisk," he said. "And there's another one. Tisk, tisk, tisk."

Carly felt as if she was being scolded.

"What do you do when you find them?" she asked.

"You grab hold and fly," said Lewis, making it sound as simple as getting on a bus.

Carly tried several times, but was unable to feel anything like what Lewis had described. "Let's just get going," she said eventually. "I have to be back at my house by morning."

"Your toes are too big," said Lewis, and flew into the treetops.

AS THEY GOT CLOSER TO the smoke, Carly walked quietly, for she kept hearing something that sounded like a whisper. She put her hand over the note in her pocket.

"It's probably just the breezes," said Lewis, but she noticed he was looking around nervously. He even tapped a tree to make sure they weren't dreaming.

Smoke began drifting through the woods around them, and Lewis perched himself on Carly's shoulder so that they wouldn't get separated.

"There it is!" he said suddenly, and Carly immediately saw it too.

It was a giant old whistle root tree on a little rise with smoke pouring out of the tips of every branch they could see.

It didn't have any leaves, and
its trunk looked almost white in
the moonlight.

"Dead trees don't normally smoke, do
they?" said Lewis, whispering in Carly's ear.

Carly was scared, but wanted to get a closer look,
and walked cautiously forward. She noticed a circle
of orange light near the base of the smoking tree and
pointed it out to Lewis.

"Stay here," he said, and flew to the ground, then got
down on all fours like a regular rat. He made no sound
and was almost impossible to see as he crept forward.

After a short time, Carly saw his dark shape appear
in front of the orange light. He stood up for a moment

and looked as though he was sniffing the air. And then he dropped back down and vanished.

"Lewis!" she said as loud as she dared, but there wasn't any answer.

She moved toward the light but stopped when she heard the whispering sound again. What was it? It didn't sound like a breeze to her.

The wind started to blow. The dead branches of the smoking whistle root tree creaked and groaned. Carly couldn't hear the whispers anymore.

She started walking forward again. She was shaking with fright. She had barely reached the spot where Lewis had disappeared when she heard something that sounded almost like laughter.

Griddle, griddle, griddle.

Carly spun around. The sound had come from behind her. Her eyes were wide and she searched the darkness for whatever had made it.

And there, sitting on a branch in a tree, was a creature that Carly had never seen before. It was covered in feathers and was grinning, and its white teeth and eyes glowed in the darkness.

The wind died down and the creature began to whisper as it stared into Carly's eyes.

"Sleep," it whispered, over and over again. "Sleep ..."

Carly's eyes closed slightly and she began to feel tired, as she did every morning when the sun rose. But she did not fall asleep.

"Sleep!" whispered the creature, a little more urgently now, and Carly saw that it wasn't grinning anymore. It climbed down the tree and walked toward her.

Carly stepped backwards. She felt clumsy. Each time the creature whispered, she felt her body weaken and her eyes start to close. But in between the whispers, she would grow stronger and more awake again.

The creature was coming faster now, and Carly turned to run. Just as she did, the creature whispered "Sleep!" again, and her legs weakened for a moment, causing her to fall.

As soon as she hit the ground, she flipped onto her back, pulled the whistle roots out of her pocket, and blew into them as hard as she could.

The sound was just as it had been at the creek that night.

The creature grabbed its ears and howled. Then it dropped to its knees and dug, pulling up clumps of dirt and stuffing them in its ears to block the sound. When that didn't work, the creature jumped sideways and scurried through the trees on all fours.

Lewis appeared then, coming out of the circle of orange light. Carly grabbed him, dropped the whistle roots back in her pocket, and ran.

"PUT ME DOWN!" SAID LEWIS, when they had run a little way. He struggled with Carly's fingers and looked prepared to bite one if he had to.

Carly placed him on the ground and hoped they

had gotten far enough away to be out of danger. She kept looking back to make sure the creature wasn't following them.

"Why did you blow those whistle roots?" demanded Lewis. "I'm surprised I haven't gone deaf."

Carly explained what had happened and about the creature she had seen, and Lewis calmed down. She asked what he'd found when he reached the circle of orange light.

It was the opening to a tunnel, he explained, and he had gone in to look around. He said it smelled as if it had been a rabbit burrow once, but he didn't think rabbits lived there now. There had been a large fire burning in the main room that was the source of the orange light and the smoke. There were rocks scattered around in there too, and something else that had surprised him most of all.

"Feathers," he said. "All over the place."

When they were almost back to the cave, they passed the white cradle and Carly stopped to check the red hat again. There was a new note inside. Carly felt her heart beating faster as she read what it said:

THE MOON CHILD IS IN DANGER

CHAPTER SEVEN

THE CRANK OF CRASSIFOLIA

ery graceful, Bitters. I didn't know dance tryouts were today."

Carly turned and saw Hetta and several of her friends standing right behind her. All of them were laughing except Hetta.

"Must be some kind of modern dance," said Hetta. She lifted a foot and moved it around in the air as Carly had been doing. "Is this right?" she asked sarcastically.

Carly's class was outside for recess and she normally would have hidden somewhere and gone to sleep. But the day was breezy and Carly had decided to practice finding tisks. So far, she hadn't had any success.

"Or maybe you're sleepwalking," said Hetta when Carly didn't answer. "But you're not really *walking,* are you? I guess you just got stuck trying to take that first step."

Carly was tempted to use the whistle roots that she now wore on a string around her neck, hidden beneath her shirt. The thought of Hetta stuffing her ears with dirt as the creature had done a couple of nights before made her smile.

Hetta looked at her in disgust. "Don't you even know when you're being made fun of, Bitters?" She pushed Carly hard, causing her to fall to the ground.

Then she stepped over her and walked away. Her friends did the same.

Carly slowly got to her feet, her smile now gone.

She had bigger things to worry about than Hetta.

She hadn't been able to stop thinking about the last message in the red hat: *The Moon Child is in danger.* Could it possibly mean her? Was it calling her the Moon Child because she was awake every night? It reminded her of what her mother used to call her — night child. But how would the hat even know who she was? She wasn't anybody special. And yet, she couldn't escape feeling that the message had been a warning — not to the rats, but to her.

She hadn't seen Lewis since their visit to the smoking whistle root tree. It had rained hard all day Wednesday and all through that night. She hadn't been able to go to the cave, and Lewis hadn't come to her rooftop.

She had sat at her window and waited for the rain to let up, but it never did. Once or twice she thought she saw a glowing white grin off in the woods, but she couldn't be sure. Did the whispering creature know where she lived?

The rain hadn't stopped until this morning, which was Thursday.

During her study period at school, she waited again at the table in the library, but Green didn't show up. Searching the dark aisle, she tried to find the book herself. She walked back and forth, running her finger over all the books she could reach.

A sudden clicking noise made Carly jump. She turned around and saw the librarian at the end of the aisle, flipping a light switch up and down.

None of the overhead lights came on.

"Someone keeps stealing the bulbs," said the librarian, looking up at the empty light sockets. "You wouldn't know who's doing it, would you, dear?"

"No, ma'am," said Carly.

"They only steal them from this aisle. A bit odd, don't you think? I'd been wondering why they don't steal them from the other aisles as well."

Carly immediately thought of Green and wondered if he was taking them to make the book harder to find, but she didn't say anything.

"And then my sister told me about a girl who likes to sleep during the day and stay up all night," continued the librarian. "That must make it very hard to go to school, wouldn't you agree?"

"Your sister, ma'am?"

"Yes, my sister. She works at the school too."

As soon as she said it, Carly saw the resemblance. The librarian had the same square head and withered-looking ears as her teacher.

Carly sighed — it was another Ms. Hankel.

"Anyway," said the second Ms. Hankel. "I thought to myself, I bet a girl like that would want to make a nice dark place where she could hide and sleep whenever she felt like it."

"I didn't take the light bulbs," said Carly, since it was clear where this conversation was going.

"I didn't say you did,

dear," answered Ms. Hankel, with the same unpleasant smile as her sister. "It's just that I've been watching you. Is there something I can help you find?"

Just then, something slammed to the ground behind Carly. She turned and saw a book in the middle of the aisle behind her.

"What was that?" asked Ms. Hankel.

"Um . . . nothing," said Carly. She bent down, picked up the book, and held it tightly to her chest. "I just dropped my book."

"I didn't see you holding a book," said Ms. Hankel suspiciously.

"I had it behind my back. It's so dark down here —it's hard to see anything." The bell rang ending the study period and Carly walked quickly around Ms. Hankel before running to her table so she could hide the book in her bag.

CARLY WANTED TO LOOK AT the book when she got back to her desk, but she felt as if she was under a spotlight with her floor lamp.

She fell asleep four times during the afternoon. Each time, Ms. Hankel blew her whistle to wake her up, though she now kept a safe distance when she did.

Carly went to bed as soon as she got home. She was worn out from trying to stay awake at school.

When she woke up, she went to the kitchen, found the bowl of buttered beans her aunt had left for her dinner, and sat down to eat with the book. She noticed immediately that it wasn't the same book Green had shown her before. But he hadn't even been in school today, so he couldn't have been the one who dropped the new book behind her.

And yet, Carly somehow knew the book was from him.

It was an old field guide to trees with a cracked black cover. She checked to see if there was an entry for whistle root trees but didn't find one. She did, however, find more pieces of old, brownish paper.

She unfolded them carefully, and this is what she read:

The CRANK of CRASSIFOLLA

The Endroot eventually became a vast forest of beautiful trees that grew nowhere else. And the boy grew into a man and lived in the forest as its king. He didn't have a castle, but that

She unfolded them carefully and read.

was of no concern to him. He loved to wander throughout his kingdom playing music for his people.

Inevitably, the five kings of the surrounding kingdoms decided they wanted the Endroot for themselves.

"He doesn't have any soldiers or weapons," said one king to the others. "We'll kill the king of Endroot and divide his forest among us."

The amber-eyed woman, whom the king of Endroot had saved as a boy, learned of their plan and went to him and took him to a place in the forest where she said he would be safe. She said he should wait there until the danger had passed.

"Play your fiddle," she told him. "They won't be able to hear you out here."

She then disguised herself as an old woman and found the kings, who were already marching through the forest. They hadn't even brought their armies. "We'll kill the king of Endroot with our own swords!" they had said to one another at a feast the night before. They had drunk great goblets of wine and toasted one another's bravery.

When they saw the old woman walking toward them, they pushed her out of their way. They had been marching all morning and their armor was growing heavy and their mood had grown sour.

"I know who you seek," said the old woman, after they had passed her by. "And I know how to find him."

The kings stopped and turned and stared at the old woman. Though none of them would have admitted it, they didn't really know where they were going. Their plan had been to march into the Endroot and kill its king. But none of them had stopped to think how they would find a king who wandered aimlessly in a vast forest and didn't have a castle.

"You'll find him by listening for his music," said the old woman, as if reading their thoughts. She cupped her hand behind her ear. "I think I hear him deeper in the forest."

The five kings listened and were surprised to hear the distant sound of a fiddle. It was very far away and they couldn't tell which direction it was coming from.

"Follow me," said the old woman, and began walking down an old path that went through what looked like some of the oldest trees in the forest.

The kings, not knowing what else to do, followed the old woman, and were pleased when they heard the sound of the fiddle growing louder.

After a long walk, the old woman finally stopped. "May I present the King of Endroot," she said, and bowed deeply, gesturing toward a whistle root tree. The kings looked and saw a man with a reddish beard sitting at the base of the tree holding a fiddle. The music had stopped and the man looked very surprised.

"If you plan to kill him," said the old woman, "at least let me give him a weapon so you can say you killed a great king instead of a poor musician."

The five kings agreed and the old woman walked toward the tree.

"What are you doing?" asked the King of

Endroot when she reached him, for he had recognized her despite her disguise. "Why have you betrayed me?"

"Trust me and do as I say," she whispered, and placed his hands on top of an oddly shaped stick that stuck straight up out of the ground. It was tall and bent at the top like a walking cane.

The five kings laughed.

"Is he going to fight us with a stick?" they asked, laughing still more. They were cruel men and drew their swords and walked forward to kill him.

"Turn the crank," whispered the disguised old woman urgently. "Do it quickly before they reach us."

The King of Endroot did as she asked and tried to turn it. It wouldn't move at first, but then to his surprise it did. He turned it round and round, even as the five kings raised their swords to strike him.

Suddenly the sound of a million bells filled the air. And the leaves of the whistle root trees began swinging back and forth even though there wasn't any wind.

The kings were about to ask the old woman what was happening when their hair and beards abruptly began to bloom, and each king soon had a lovely mane of white flowers. Their toes began to grow, right through the tips of their boots, and dug into the ground like roots. They dropped their swords and felt their raised arms hardening into the branches they would soon become. Little green leaves sprouted at the tips of their fingers and the forest suddenly had five new trees where the kings had formerly stood.

The woman's name was Crassifolia, and the oddly shaped stick became known as the Crank of Crassifolia. The King of Endroot turned it whenever there was danger, and the whistle root trees never failed to protect his kingdom during the long and peaceful years of his reign.

WHEN SHE HAD FINISHED READING, Carly folded the papers and placed them back in the book. Her mind was racing with thoughts of the Endroot and whistle root trees. Had she found a way to save the rats?

She quietly opened the kitchen door that led outside. She listened for whispers and looked for glowing grins in the dark, but didn't hear or see either. She also didn't see any owls. Still, she made sure she had her whistle roots before she closed the door and took off running through the woods with the book clasped in her arms.

"WHAT ARE YOU DOING HERE?" asked Lewis angrily when she reached the cave a short time later.

What is the matter with him? Carly wondered, but then she saw that he was holding his fiddle. Lewis was never patient when he wanted to play music, and he always wanted to play. Without the rules that kept him from playing by himself, he'd probably never stop.

"I was just coming to your rooftop," he said. "And now it's going to take forever to get back there." He looked sadly at her toes, as if wishing they were smaller and better able to find tisks.

"But I've found something, Lewis," said Carly, holding the book out to him and trying to catch her breath. "And I have to show Breeza Meezy."

Lewis sighed and made a halfhearted gesture toward the tower. He had dismissed the warnings from the hat as nonsense, and Carly feared he would do the same to her plan. He seemed to still believe that the owls would start dancing again if he just kept playing music for them.

Carly hoped Breeza Meezy would see things differently.

As she walked through the village, she noticed that half the houses no longer had light in the windows. It was so sad how many rats had been taken by the owls or drowned by the rising creek. It was even sadder to think what would happen if she couldn't save the rats who remained. This little magical world she had just discovered would disappear forever.

When she reached the tower, she bent down and knocked on it gently and then stood back to wait. Breeza Meezy appeared a few moments later.

"Good evening, my dear," she said, gesturing for Carly to sit down in the wooden chair.

Carly bowed slightly and said good evening and sat down. "I've

found another story," she said. "It's about the whistle root trees, like the story I told you before. May I read it to you?"

"Of course."

When Carly had finished reading, she placed the papers back in the book and gently closed it. "I think we should try to find the Crank," she said.

Breeza Meezy looked at her in confusion. "But it's just a story — isn't it, dear?"

"I don't know," admitted Carly. "But this is the only place in the world where whistle root trees grow. What if these woods used to be the Kingdom of Endroot? That would mean the Crank could still be here."

Breeza Meezy looked out over the village toward the cave opening where the old whistle root tree stood.

"Even if it is here and we could find it," she said, "what would happen if we turned it?"

"Maybe the owls would go back to dancing in the trees!" said Carly.

"Or be turned *into* trees!" said Breeza Meezy with alarm.

Carly was again surprised by how concerned Breeza Meezy was for the owls despite everything they had done to the rats.

"The creek never rose," said Breeza Meezy abruptly, before Carly had a chance to say anything else. "It rained all day and night and the creek never rose. And it's never risen before, at least as far back as I can remember. And on the night when the village flooded, there hadn't been any rain for weeks."

Carly thought back to that night. Why hadn't she thought of that before? What *had* caused the creek to rise?

"It could rise again," continued Breeza Meezy. "Without warning. And more rats could be lost. There's nothing we could do to stop it. And the owls have taken so many of us already . . . our musicians are all but gone."

Carly looked up and saw Lewis sitting on his roof, holding his fiddle and looking forlorn.

"I've decided to move the village," said Breeza Meezy. "Somewhere away from the creek. Probably away from these woods altogether."

"What?" said Carly, taken completely by surprise

and getting to her feet. "But you can't! Where would you go?"

"I've sent scouts to find a new cave," said Breeza Meezy. "They're flying through the woods as we speak."

"But the owls will get them!" said Carly, worried that more rats could be lost.

"They're traveling together in a group of five," explained Breeza Meezy. "Each rat is carrying a whistle root and they'll blow them together if they're attacked by owls. That should keep them safe."

"But you can't leave the woods!" said Carly, and heard how sorrowful her voice sounded. She knew she was being selfish, but how could she go back to the lonely nights she had known before meeting Lewis?

Breeza Meezy was quiet for a moment and then asked, "Have there been any more notes in the cradle?"

Carly took a breath and told her what the last two notes had said. Breeza Meezy seemed especially interested in the one that mentioned the Moon Child being in danger.

"Do you think it could mean me?" Carly asked suddenly.

Breeza Meezy stared at her thoughtfully. "Perhaps," she said. "As far as I know, you are the first person to sit in that chair since the Moon King himself. And you are awake every night, clearly governed more by the moon than the sun. If there is a Moon Child in these woods, it seems likely that it's you."

CHAPTER EIGHT

GRANNY PITCHER'S CABIN

The next day, Carly set a trap in the library.

She was so tired that she knew she would fall asleep in class anyway, so she decided to spend her day on the bottom shelf of a bookcase.

It was a simple plan really.

She had gotten to school early and had snuck in to the library, making sure that Ms. Hankel didn't see her. She had placed the book back in the middle of the dark aisle exactly where she had found it. She had then cleared the books off one of the bottom shelves nearby and had made enough room for herself to lie down. From there, she could still see the book, but no one looking down the aisle would be able to see her.

Ms. Hankel had been right, Carly realized. With

the light bulbs gone, this was the perfect spot for her to hide and sleep.

She watched the book, waiting to see what would happen. She found that the darkness actually helped her stay awake, despite how tired she was.

But when nothing happened during the first hour, she eventually did fall asleep, even though she didn't want to.

CARLY'S EYES FLEW OPEN AND she banged her head on the shelf above her.

Something had woken her up.

She looked where the book should have been, but it was gone, and she scrambled out of her shelf and looked around.

Almost immediately, she noticed something she hadn't seen before — all of the bottom shelves against the wall were completely filled with books except for one, which was only half filled.

She bent down and grabbed one of the books. But when she did, all of the other books came out with it.

Someone had glued them together.

She got down on her hands and knees and saw that behind the books was a hole in the wall. And in that hole was what appeared to be the top of a ladder. She stuck her head in and looked down, but it was too dark to see what was at the bottom.

She would have to go in backwards if she wanted to climb down. She hesitated for a moment, but then heard Ms. Hankel.

"Who's over there?" said Ms. Hankel, her voice coming closer. "If I catch whoever's stealing those bulbs, I'll slap their ears till they fall off!"

Quickly, Carly backed into the hole and found the rungs of the ladder with her feet. She climbed down a bit, and then grabbed the glued-together books and pulled them back into place in front of the hole.

"What happened to these books?" she heard Ms. Hankel ask angrily.

Carly held her breath. She assumed that librarians frowned on books being glued together. She imagined Ms. Hankel tossing them aside and dragging her out of the hole by her ears like a rabbit.

But nothing happened. And after a few minutes, Carly pushed the books slightly to the side and peeked out.

Ms. Hankel was on the other side of the aisle. She was putting the books back on the bottom shelf that Carly had cleared for her hiding place.

Safe for the moment, Carly looked down toward the bottom of the hole. She knew that whoever had taken the book had gone down there. And so, slowly and quietly, she began to climb down.

When she reached the bottom, she couldn't see a thing. She felt around with her hands and found that she was in a small space with four walls. Three of the walls felt like bricks. The other one felt like wood.

Not knowing what else to do, she knocked on the wood wall.

Suddenly, the wood wall disappeared.

"What are you doing here?" a familiar voice asked her.

Two hands reached in and pulled her into a dimly lit room. She looked back and saw that she had stepped out of a fireplace. She looked to her right and saw Green holding her arm.

"What are *you* doing here?" Carly asked him. "Under the library, I mean."

Green looked embarrassed and didn't say anything. He let go of her arm and concentrated on putting the wood board back in front of the fireplace.

Carly studied the room.

There were several lanterns hanging from wood beams in the ceiling, which appeared to be the only source of light. An ancient rug covered the center of the floor. There was also a table, an old couch, a sink, a stove, a cupboard, and a bed piled high with blankets.

And by the fireplace, a lonely little chair sat by itself with a book lying on its seat.

"Do you *live* here?" asked Carly.

Green nodded and stared at the floor.

"I mean, it's all right if you do," said Carly. "I promise I won't tell anyone."

She reached out and touched one of the walls; the stones felt cool and damp. She understood why Green needed the blankets, since there was a definite chill in the room.

"How did you build this?" she asked with real admiration in her voice.

"I didn't. My grandmother did. It was a cabin she built for herself."

"But why did she build it down here?"

"Well, it wasn't under the school when she built it. It was in a little valley between two small hills."

Carly was confused, so Green walked over to a small desk she hadn't seen and opened one of the drawers. He took out a newspaper and handed it to Carly.

On the front page of an old copy of the *Whistle Root Gazette*, Carly read the headline:

GRANNY PITCHER LOSES FIGHT TO SAVE HOME — TOWN SEIZES PROPERTY TO BUILD NEW SCHOOL

*"Do you live *here*?" asked Carly.*

There was a black-and-white picture under the headline of a fierce-looking old woman standing in front of a little cabin. She looked ready to hit the camera with the block of firewood she held in her raised right hand. In her left arm she held a baby.

"Neither of the two small hills was big enough for them to build the school on," explained Green. "So they filled the valley up with dirt and built the school on top. They were supposed to tear the cabin down — but I guess they were in a rush, because they just poured dirt on top of it. And when Granny found out the cabin was still there she . . . well, she moved back in."

The pile of blankets coughed and Carly jumped backwards in surprise.

"That's Granny," said Green, and walked over to the bed. He pulled the blankets down a bit and Carly could see the long gray hair of a very old woman.

"Is she okay?" asked Carly.

"She's been sick for a few weeks now," said Green. He put his hand gently on her head, and then walked over to the little kitchen and stirred something in a pot on the stove. "I guess you were watching when I took the book," he said, and Carly suddenly felt guilty about tricking him into revealing his secret.

"I'm sorry, Green," she said. "But I wanted to find you. You've been gone for days."

Green turned to look at her and pushed his glasses back up his nose. In the unsteady light from the lanterns, his red hair flickered like an unkempt fire.

"I guess we're even," he said. "Since I got you into trouble with Ms. Hankel." He nodded toward a corner of the room and Carly saw a box filled with the missing light bulbs. "I thought it would make it easier to come and go during the day, so I could check on Granny without anybody seeing me. But I've been so worried that I haven't wanted to leave her alone."

Carly looked again at the picture in the newspaper.

"Is the baby you?" she asked.

"Yes. Granny took me in when my parents died."

Carly looked up at Green. "My parents are gone too."

They were both silent for a moment. Then, feeling awkward, Carly turned away and studied the room a little more. She saw a regular-looking door and windows with shutters closed over them. She wondered what she'd see if she opened them. She kept looking around and jumped when she saw an owl staring at her. The owl was very still and stood on a tall perch in a corner of the room.

"You have a pet owl?" she asked, trying to keep the fear out of her voice.

"What? Oh, that's just Elzick. He was Granny's. He lived with us for years. And Granny loved him so much that she stuffed him when he died. I forget he's there sometimes."

There was a pile of books beneath Elzick, and Green saw where she was looking.

"I haven't found any more yet," he said. "Stories, I mean. But you can look through those books if you'd like. You might get lucky and find one."

Carly walked cautiously toward Elzick and sat down. She picked up a book from the pile and flipped through the pages but didn't find anything.

"How do you know which books to look in?" she asked.

"I don't," said Green. "I found the first one in the library by accident, during the summer. And then

I got curious and wondered if there were more, so I started looking and found the second one. But I haven't found any more since then. And now Ms. Hankel has convinced the school to hire a night watchman, and he's always hanging out in the library, so the best I can do is grab a bunch of books whenever I get a chance and bring them down here."

Carly looked through a second, and a third, and a fourth book but still didn't find anything.

"Do you think the stories are true?" she asked as she reached for another book.

"Granny said they are," said Green. "She told me to show them to you . . . before she got sick."

Carly looked up.

"What do you mean? She knows who I am?"

"I guess so."

Carly looked toward the bed.

"But I never met her. Why would she want *me* to see them?"

Green shrugged. He was holding two steaming bowls. "Do you want something to eat?"

Carly walked to the table and sat down, still wondering why Green's grandmother would have wanted her to see the stories.

Carly looked in her bowl and saw that Green had made pea soup. He had also put a small loaf of bread on the table for them to share.

"If you like the food in the cafeteria, you'll love this," he said. He broke off a piece of bread and dipped it in his soup.

"You stole this?"

"I had to. Granny and I used to gather what we ate from the woods at night. But since she got sick . . . well, it's just a lot quicker to get food from the cafeteria."

"When *did* she get sick?" asked Carly.

"About three weeks ago, I guess," said Green. "I found her one night, sleeping, and she hasn't woken up since then."

Carly inhaled sharply and her eyes opened wide.

"What's wrong?" asked Green. "Are you okay?"

"Yes, it's just . . . I don't think your grandmother's sick, Green."

"What do you mean?"

Carly hesitated for a moment, but then she told him about the smoking whistle root tree and the whispering creature covered in feathers. She told him how it had tried to make her sleep.

To her surprise, Green didn't laugh and tell her she was crazy.

"You said you heard it *griddle?*" he asked.

Carly nodded. "It sounded like laughter."

Green was quiet for a moment. "It's funny, but it reminds me of something Granny used to tell me. She said a griddlebeast lived in these woods — though what that was she never explained. But she told me to run if I ever saw an animal I didn't recognize, and to never let it speak to me. It scared me when I was little, but when I got older, I thought she'd just made it up . . . you know, to keep me from wandering too far into the woods by myself. I'd almost forgotten about it until now."

Carly and Green heard the sound of school bells ringing above them.

"But if there *is* a griddlebeast," said Carly, "and that's what I saw, and it's been here all this time, why hasn't it done anything before now?"

"Maybe it has. How would we know? Granny's out in the woods at night a lot. Maybe she just got unlucky and ran into it." Green paused, looking at Carly. "Has anything *else* strange happened lately?"

Carly thought about the rats and how they were disappearing. She thought about their village and the creek that had risen mysteriously and almost destroyed it. She thought about the warnings from the red hat. Feeling certain she could trust Green, she began to tell him everything: about Lewis and the rats, about the cave and the creek, about the owls and the whistle roots, and about the white cradle and the hat.

And the whole time she talked, she couldn't escape the feeling that Elzick was watching her.

CHAPTER NINE

THE GRIDDLEBEAST

arly had indeed seen a griddlebeast at the smoking whistle root tree.

Several weeks before the rats began disappearing, the griddlebeast had hatched from a rock in a small field filled with other rocks much like his. He knocked on several of them, but there wasn't any answer, so he said his farewells and walked into the woods.

He was hungry that first night and crawled down a hole and ate an entire family of rabbits. He liked their burrow very much and decided it would make an excellent home. It smelled of rabbits, but that didn't bother him. He rather liked the smell of rabbits — it made him think of food.

He furnished the burrow completely with rocks. They were, after all, the closest thing to family that he had. They weren't comfortable, but he rarely had company. And when he did have company it was normally rabbits, and he was planning to eat them anyway, so it really didn't matter if they spent a few uncomfortable moments sitting on some rocks.

He decided rabbits tasted best if you cooked them first, so he kept a fire burning and dug a hole in the ceiling so that the burrow wouldn't fill with smoke. He dug straight upward into the bottom of a whistle root tree, which he completely hollowed out, right to the tips of its smallest branches. He cut holes there, so that the smoke could escape, and turned the entire tree into a giant chimney that looked constantly on the verge of bursting into flames.

The rabbits were easy to catch. He snuck up on them in the fields while they were eating and whispered in their ears. "Follow me," he whispered, and surprisingly they did, whole groups of them at a time, like little ducks following their mother.

The griddlebeast could have gone on this way quite pleasantly, eating rabbits and growing fat. But one moonlit night he heard the rats playing music and suddenly knew that he had been placed in these woods for a reason.

He would be very busy now, he realized, but he looked forward to it, almost as much as he looked forward to eating rabbits. "Oh, wonderful night!" he said, and spread his arms wide to the trees and stars above, and laughed happily, saying, *"Griddle, griddle, griddle . . ."*

He found the first owl sleeping in a tree early the next day. "Take the rats," he whispered to the dreaming owl. He whispered it several times, and then

climbed down the tree and hurried away through the woods. He found other sleeping owls and whispered the same words to each of them. "Take the rats," he said. He liked to steal a few feathers from each owl and stick them in his fur.

By the time the griddlebeast had found all the owls in the woods, he was so covered in feathers that he looked almost like an owl himself.

The griddlebeast's body is shaped like an upright bloated bean. His hands and feet look like delicate, long-legged spiders. He's as tall as a tree stump. His small, pointed ears sit on top of his small round head. He walks on two skinny legs. He runs on all fours. He grins unpleasantly. He whispers when he talks.

He saw the old woman in the woods one night. He followed her home and whispered "Sleep" through a keyhole. She never even knew he was there.

And on the night of the flood, he walked along the little creek until he was quite close to the rats' cave. He got down on all fours and drank from the creek, like a cat licking up milk from a bowl.

When he was no longer thirsty, he stopped drinking and looked at himself in the gently flowing water.

He was still wearing the owl feathers and he liked the way they looked in his fur.

He then began to whisper again.

"Rise," he whispered to the creek. "Rise, rise, rise!"

He raised his arms and danced in a circle excitedly.

CHAPTER TEN

A RISKY TISK

It was late Friday night.

Carly stared out her window at the new squash. The moon was out and she knew Lewis would be along soon. She had already seen owls flying nearby. She wished she could blow her whistle roots to scare them off, but she didn't want to wake her aunt or the neighbors.

Carly was quietly playing a small piano that her aunt let her keep in her room. She was playing short lines of music her father had written. The piano had belonged to him, and Carly had found the music, written on scraps of paper, in a storage space in the piano bench several years ago.

Sometimes she imagined she could hear messages in the tunes when she played — that her parents loved her, that they missed her . . . though she knew it was foolish to think the tunes were saying anything at all.

She stopped playing and instead thought about every-thing Green had told her ear-lier that day. She felt certain she had seen a griddlebeast at the smoking whistle root tree. What else could it have been? And she thought about the griddlebeast's whispers and how powerful they were. She wondered how she had stayed awake when Green's grand-mother could not.

But really, she already knew the answer. Whatever was inside her that kept her awake every night, and resisted the most powerful sleeping pills her doctor could prescribe, had also been able to resist the grid-dlebeast's whispers. Though she didn't know what would happen if the griddlebeast caught her in the daylight.

Carly stared out at the woods. Was this once the Kingdom of Endroot?

Just then, Lewis climbed up over the edge of the roof holding his fiddle.

"Why didn't you fly up here?" she asked when she opened her window.

"It's too windy," he said.

Carly hadn't noticed but the wind was blowing strongly.

"You can't fly when it's windy?"

"No, not in wind like this," said Lewis. "I'd probably end up miles from where I wanted to go. And that's only if I didn't get killed crashing into a tree or something."

Carly thought of her father and the tornado that killed him. She knew how dangerous the wind could be. Nevertheless, she crawled out her window onto the roof.

"Hold this," said Lewis, and handed her his fiddle. He checked her fingers to make sure she was holding it correctly, not too tight and not too loose, and then disappeared back over the edge of the roof. When he climbed back up, he was holding a drum, which he placed beside the new squash.

"Where did all the rules come from?" Carly asked him.

"What rules?" said Lewis.

"The rule about having to use a vegetable when a

band loses one of its members — and the rule about always playing with three instruments — and the rules about only playing in moonlight and always playing up high. Those rules," said Carly. "They don't make much sense."

Lewis shrugged. "They're just rules."

"And why didn't Breeza Meezy stop the musicians from playing when the owls began taking them?" she continued. "She could have saved them. But now they're all gone and you're the only one left. Doesn't that bother you?"

Lewis looked at her with disbelief and anger in his eyes.

"We have *always* played our music," he said with great pride in his voice. He snatched his fiddle back from her and played a few angry notes.

"But couldn't you have made an exception? At least for a little while? Just until you'd figured out how to make the owls start dancing again?"

"None of the musicians would have agreed to that!" said Lewis, his face jutting forward and his tail whipping around in the air behind him.

Carly had not intended to anger Lewis. She just had so many questions and couldn't seem to get answers to any of them. She looked away from his stare and idly lifted her hand to feel the wind run under her palm.

And it was then that she felt her first tisk.

It was so subtle, just a little bump under one of her fingertips. She tried again and felt another one — a dent this time. Was she really feeling them?

She kept her hand out, and when she felt the next tisk, she pushed down just the slightest bit with her finger and was instantly yanked forward. She let go, but was curious and tried again. And before she could release the next tisk, she was off the roof and flying over the lawn.

It felt as if she had grabbed the tail of a runaway horse. The lawn passed beneath her and she found herself flying over the woods.

She was completely out of control. The wind pulled her up toward the moon and then sent her diving toward the trees. It seemed that the wind was trying to shake her loose, so violent were its twists and turns.

She didn't dare let go; the fall would surely kill her.

Suddenly, she felt something slam into the back of her head and grab her hair.

"Have you gone mad?" she heard Lewis's voice say in her ear.

The wind pulled her up toward the moon.

He crawled quickly down to her shoulder, and then out her arm toward the finger that was holding the tisk.

"Try and grab as many tisks as you can!" he yelled to her. "Use both of your hands and all of your fingers!"

Carly did as he said and stretched the fingers and thumb of the hand that was holding the tisk as far as they would go, trying to feel the little bumps and dents. She could only find a couple more. With her other hand, she felt around more freely and grabbed three tisks that were right next to each other — two bumps and a dent.

"I think I've got all I can!" she yelled to Lewis.

He crawled to the edge of her hand and looked like a parachutist about to jump from a plane. He reached out with one foot and felt around with his toes until he found a tisk. He then stepped from Carly's hand into the wind and found a few more with his other foot.

"Try to steer it downward!" he yelled. "Now!"

Carly pushed down on the tisks and was surprised when she and Lewis dropped straight toward the trees. They were going much too fast — they were going to crash!

"Not so hard!" yelled Lewis.

Carly panicked and lifted her fingers and lost all of the tisks except one. The wind yanked them back upward and shook them both back and forth. Carly felt as if her arm was going to be pulled out of its socket.

"Grab the tisks again!" yelled Lewis.

Carly did as he said and found the tisks more quickly this time.

"Now steer downward again, but don't push so hard!" he commanded.

Carly pushed down on the tisks more gently than before. And she and Lewis plunged back downward, but at more of an angle this time.

"Now when we get close to the trees, lift your fingers slowly and try and fly right above them!" yelled Lewis. "There's a meadow up ahead! We'll try and land there!"

Carly watched the tops of the trees coming at them fast. Just before they hit them, she lifted her fingers the slightest bit. But she either didn't lift them enough, or the wind had a mind of its own, because they crashed into the uppermost leaves and branches of the trees.

Carly grabbed Lewis with her left hand and flung her right arm out to grab whatever she could find. She caught the end of a long branch and wrapped her fingers tightly around it and held on with all the strength she had.

The branch bent with Carly and Lewis dangling on its end. Carly looked down and could barely see the ground in the darkness.

They both heard snapping noises. The branch was breaking! Right at the point where it connected to the trunk of the tree. Carly screamed and imagined breaking into pieces when she hit the ground, as if she were made of glass.

But the branch broke slowly. And with each snapping noise, they dropped just a little more, as the branch broke bit by bit, lowering them gently through the air.

In the end, Carly's feet touched lightly on the ground and she let go of the branch, like a small child letting go of a parent's hand. She looked around and saw that her feet were surrounded by whistle roots.

They had been saved by a whistle root tree.

"What were you thinking?" said Lewis angrily. "Hadn't I just told you how dangerous it is to fly on the wind?"

"I didn't mean to," said Carly. "I wasn't even trying

to find a tisk when it happened. It was just there suddenly, under my fingertip. And I only pressed down
slightly. I had no idea it was going to pull me off the
roof like that!"

Lewis crossed his arms and scowled at her.

"Thanks for coming after me," she said sincerely.
"I might have been killed if you hadn't. Or ended up
who knows where — on the moon for all I know." The
thought frightened her so badly, she resolved never to
fly on the wind again.

Lewis waved away her thank-you.

"Well, I couldn't let that happen, could I?" he said.
"It's like I told you before, it would be a great embarrassment to have two vegetables in the band. And be-
sides, where would I find a squash that can play the
horn as well as you?"

Carly had to smile. She knew that for Lewis, that
was the highest compliment he could have given her.

BECAUSE THE WIND HAD TAKEN them up and
down so much, they weren't that far from Carly's
house. Walking back through the woods, Carly was
glad she always wore her whistle roots now — in case
they saw any owls, or even worse, the griddlebeast.

Aside from those dangers, she was also looking for anything that could be the Crank of Crassifolia. If it existed and she turned it, could the rats be saved? Would Green's grandmother wake up? And what about Carly? She hadn't forgotten the last message in the red hat. If she *was* the Moon Child, whatever that meant, would the Crank protect her? What danger was she in exactly?

She had asked Green if he thought the woods had once been the Kingdom of Endroot.

"Maybe," he'd said. "But it seems odd that a whole kingdom could have been forgotten."

Carly tried turning a few small, crooked trees, but nothing happened. When Lewis asked her what she was doing, she quickly thought of an answer.

"Checking for shimmer trees," she said.

She couldn't tell him the truth. He would be against turning the Crank just as Breeza Meezy had been. And for the same reason — he wouldn't want the owls to suffer the same fate as the five kings in the Endroot.

But what if turning the Crank was the only way to stop the griddlebeast too?

Carly knew the griddlebeast had whispered Green's grandmother into her endless sleep. And she suspected it was also behind the owl attacks and the rising creek.

Was that also done with whispers?

CARLY AND LEWIS'S PATH HOME took them by the cradle, and Carly checked the red hat as she always did. There was a new note inside. It said:

THE BELLS MUST RING!

Immediately she knew that it meant the whistle root trees. But how could she make them ring?

And who is sending me these messages? she wondered, not for the first time.

Suddenly she had an idea.

Maybe she could send a message back.

WHEN THEY GOT TO CARLY'S roof, the wind died down and Lewis played his fiddle. Carly played her horn with him, but she was really watching warily for owls and thinking about what to say in the message.

When it was almost sunrise, Lewis promised to see her the next night and then flew away on a breeze. Carly closed her window and sat down at her desk to write.

Dear Note Sender,

HOW do I make the whistle root trees ring? WHERE is the Crank of Crassifolia? Does it still exist? Much confusion and suffering here due to constant owl attacks. If I can't find the Crank, what else should I do? Please respond soon. A long letter (or at least more than one sentence) would be appreciated.

Yours truly,

Carly Bean Bitters

It was growing light outside and Carly felt her eyelids beginning to droop. It was Saturday morning and it had been an exhausting week. She wanted to run to the cradle and put her note in the hat, but she was afraid she would fall asleep in the woods.

She checked to make sure the window was locked and began to walk to her bed. But she had forgotten to shut the curtains and sunlight suddenly poured in and lit up her room with a blinding brightness.

Carly blinked once, as one would in response to a camera flash, and was asleep before she even hit the floor.

WHEN SHE WOKE UP, IT was already night again. Her aunt had obviously been in her room, since Carly was now lying on her bed and there was a cold lump of squash casserole in a bowl on her night table. Carly knew it was ridiculous, but she went to the window and closed her curtains so that the squash on her roof couldn't see her eating it.

Maybe I have gone crazy, she thought. It was a possibility that had crossed her mind before.

After she finished eating, she made herself a cup of tea. And while it cooled, she prepared to take her bowl downstairs so she could put it in the kitchen sink. It was then that she saw the envelope. It was propped against her lamp and addressed to her, but it didn't have a return address or stamp, so someone must have delivered it. There was a note in her aunt's handwriting on it that said:

FOUND THIS IN THE MAILBOX.
FOUND YOU ON THE FLOOR. THE
SCHOOL CALLED. SOMETHING
ABOUT YOU STEALING LIGHT
    BULBS AND HITTING A
    TEACHER?

Carly groaned, but calls from the school were nothing new. Her aunt had been getting them almost weekly since Carly's first day of kindergarten, when she had fallen asleep going down a slide on the playground. It had happened when she was about halfway down, and her limp little body had slid the rest of the way and dropped into the dirt without making a sound. The teacher thought she had died and had run to the nurse's office screaming. And there had been so many calls since then that her aunt rarely even talked to her about them anymore.

Carly opened the envelope and read the letter inside.

Can you come to the school tonight? I've found something you should see. Meet me at the outside cafeteria door by the trash bins. Around eight? I don't know what time you wake up. —Green

CARLY LOOKED AT THE CLOCK; she was already late. She jumped out of bed and ran to the window and opened it. Then she remembered the note she'd written and grabbed it from her desk before jumping out the window onto the roof.

When she reached the cradle, she checked the red hat. There wasn't a new message, so she placed her note inside and then ran all the way to the school.

Green wasn't there when she reached the cafeteria door. She whispered his name a few times, but there was no answer. She found a candle and a box of matches on top of a trash can, along with a note from him that said the door was unlocked and to meet him in the library.

It was very dark inside the school and she was thankful for the candle. She cupped her hand around the flame to keep it from making too much light. She remembered what Green had said about the watchman.

She made her way through the kitchen and into the cafeteria itself, and then out into the hallway that led to the library.

"You're here!" said Green excitedly, as he removed the wood board from the front of the fireplace. He walked over to the pile of books on the floor beneath Elzick. "The watchman fell asleep, so I had a chance to search the library again and found this . . ." He picked up a book from the top of the pile and handed it to Carly.

It was another old book with a thick, dusty cover. Carly opened it and flipped through the pages. When she found the pieces of brownish paper, she could hardly contain her excitement. She unfolded them, read the title, and looked up at Green with wide, surprised eyes.

He had found the story of the Moon King.

CHAPTER ELEVEN

THE MOON KING

The MOON KING

The King of Endroot lived to be a hundred years old. And to the end of his life, he loved and cared for the forest he had planted as a boy.

He had no need of armies because of the protection of the whistle root trees. He had no need of castles because the forest was his home. And in his old age, his fiddle became his voice and his final words before he died were not spoken but played.

"The Moon Child is in danger," is what his final tune had said, although most everyone listening heard only music.

The message was understood by no one

except his youngest son. The boy did not tell anyone what he had heard. It had been a warning, perhaps for his ears alone. For he had the oddest affliction. His clock was reversed. He slept during the day and was awake all night. And he knew that it was he to whom the tune was referring.

The king's eleven other sons assumed that the oldest would now be king, something which the oldest son assumed as well. He did not care for music or the forest, and when his father died, he began to build the castle of which he had always dreamed.

Trees were chopped down. The people were forced to work day and night.

And then, everything stopped.

A decree had been found hidden inside the old king's fiddle; the final decree from the King of Endroot.

"My youngest son shall be the next king" was all that it said, but it was enough. And the oldest brother was forced to step down from his throne so that the boy could sit there instead.

Almost immediately, rumors began to spread.

"Why is he only awake at night?" the people asked each other suspiciously.

"I'll tell you why," said the oldest brother whenever he heard people talking like this. "It's the time of witchery, that's why."

He took every opportunity to help the suspicions of the people grow.

He was eventually so successful in this that the people revolted and took the boy while he was sleeping and threw him in the dungeon. It was the only part of the castle that had been completed. And now that the oldest brother was king again, he wasted no time in forcing the people back to work.

From a dark and damp cell deep within the earth, the boy could hear his brother's castle being built on top of him.

"Find the witch Crassifolia," the new king commanded his brothers. "And kill her if she still lives." No one had seen her for many years, but he did not want to take any chances. And just to be sure that his throne would not be taken from him again, he gave one more order.

"Chop down the whistle root trees," he said. Although he was selfish and cruel, he was also a smart man and had little doubt that it would be he who would suffer if someone turned the Crank. His father had never told him where it was, and he was certain that Crassifolia would never reveal its location to him either.

To make sure his order was carried out, he issued a decree stating that anyone who refused to chop down whistle root trees would be chopped into pieces themselves.

When the first whistle root tree came down, a door was made from its wood, which was placed in front of the boy's cell. The guards in the dungeon loved to taunt the boy, and carved the words "Moon King" into it to amuse themselves and mock him further.

The boy lived in that cell for the next three years. When he finally escaped, he saw something he knew would have broken his father's heart.

Every whistle root tree in the Kingdom of
Endroot was gone.

"'THE MOON CHILD IS IN danger,'" said Carly when
she finished reading the story. "Those are the exact
words in one of the notes I found in the red hat. I had
thought it was referring to me."

"It probably was," said Green. "The story must
have taken place a long time ago. You *are* the Moon
Child now. You're just like he was, awake at night and
asleep during the day."

"And they called him the Moon King to make fun
of him," she said sadly, thinking of him sitting alone
in the dungeon for all those years. "He was only a boy.
He could have been *our* age. And they chopped down
the whistle root trees too — which is terrible — but
which also means that these woods weren't once the
Kingdom of Endroot — which means that there is no
Crank of Crassifolia — which means that I have no
idea how to save the rats or your grandmother!"

Carly felt so terrible that she almost regretted having read the story.

"There must be more stories," said Green quickly,
seeing how upset she was. "I'll find them. I'll look

every chance I get. And maybe we missed something in one of the other stories, maybe there's some clue, something that would tell us how to make the whistle root trees ring without the Crank."

Green pulled out the other two stories and they read them again but didn't find anything new. They also kept checking on Green's grandmother, who was very restless. They tried to wake her but nothing worked. And when it was very late, Green fell asleep and Carly sat on Granny Pitcher's bed the rest of the night, held her hand, and spoke softly to calm her, just in case she could hear.

An hour or so before sunrise, Carly woke Green and said that she should go. She started walking toward the fireplace.

"Why don't you use the front door?" said Green with a smile.

Carly had imagined that there would be just a wall of dirt behind it. But when Green got up and opened the door, she saw a dark tunnel instead.

"It leads to our garden in the woods," he said. "Granny and I dug it out over the years. C'mon." He grabbed two candles and lit them and handed one to Carly.

The tunnel was tall enough that they could walk without stooping. But large tree roots poked through the dirt in the ceiling and walls, and Carly jumped every time one brushed against her.

"So if this was never the Kingdom of Endroot, how do you think the whistle root trees got here?" she asked Green as they made their way through the dark passage.

"I don't know," he said. "But however they got here, they've been here a very long time. Granny told me they're hundreds of years old. But even she didn't know where they came from — or at least she never told me."

Carly suddenly thought of an answer. "The boy must have brought them!" she said. "The Moon King! He must have come here, somehow, after he got out of the dungeon! That's how the rats know about him.

They even have this old chair that Breeza Meezy told me was his. He must have planted the whistle root trees here just as his father had planted them in the Endroot!"

They had stopped walking and stood facing each other in the dark tunnel.

"That *has* to be it!" said Green.

"But I guess knowing that doesn't help us very much, does it?" said Carly. "It doesn't tell us how to make the whistle root trees ring."

"True," said Green. "But it's still important."

They continued walking and finally reached the end of the tunnel. There was a ladder there.

When Carly looked up, she saw a door in the ceiling above their heads.

"This is where I found Granny," said Green. "She was here at the bottom of the ladder. I had to pull her through the tunnel back to the cabin." He climbed up the ladder and unlocked the door with a large old-fashioned key. He then pushed it open and Carly could suddenly see stars.

Green climbed through the opening and Carly followed right behind him. She found herself in a small clearing in the woods. At first, it looked as if she was surrounded by weeds. But as she looked closer, she saw that it was a carefully disguised garden. There were no orderly rows of vegetables or pleasant little fences here. Everything was in disarray and planted without any sort of pattern that would attract attention. Someone could walk right through it and never even notice it was a garden at all.

"Granny's very secretive," said Green, an explanation that was probably unnecessary given that they had just walked through a tunnel from a cabin hidden under a school to get here.

Carly noticed the moonlight shining on the skin of a squash and felt as if her heart had stopped beating.

Moonlight!

"I have to go!" she told Green. "Do you know which way my neighborhood is?"

Green thought for a moment.

"It's that way," he said, and pointed east.

"I'll see you Monday at school," she yelled, and took off running. She heard Green ask if something was wrong, but she didn't have time to stop and answer him.

She ran through the woods, desperate to reach her house. When she finally got there, and had climbed up the young oak tree onto her roof, she saw exactly what she had feared.

The squash was there, as always, with the drum beside it. But now there was also an onion with a horn propped against it that wasn't hers.

A band had to have three members, and she hadn't been there when Lewis came to her rooftop tonight.

He had told her once that it would be a great embarrassment to have two vegetables in the band, but he had clearly done just that.

How determined he must have been to play his fiddle, regardless of the danger. With the moon still in the night sky, Carly knew he'd be there yet, unless something had happened.

Even as the owls swooped down on him, Lewis wouldn't have stopped playing. And he must have held his fiddle tightly when they carried him away, for it was nowhere to be seen.

Carly couldn't stop the tears that were falling onto her cheeks and nose.

Lewis was gone.

CHAPTER TWELVE

TREE RINGS

e was the last musician," said Breeza Meezy when Carly told her about Lewis the next night. "There is no reason for us to stay in these woods any longer."

She told Carly that the scouts had found a new cave, far from the whistle root trees and on high enough ground that they would never have to worry about flooding again.

Carly had come to see Breeza Meezy as soon as she had woken up. She couldn't bear to stay in her room.

She hadn't even eaten the dinner her aunt had left for her. She hadn't been hungry. She had only felt tired, something that she never felt at night.

She missed Lewis terribly and had convinced herself that his death was her fault.

He had told her he was coming to her rooftop. Why

hadn't she thought about him before leaving her room last night?

"We should be ready to leave tomorrow," said Breeza Meezy, interrupting her thoughts.

"But how will you move the houses and tower?" asked Carly. She desperately wanted the rats to stay, but she couldn't ask them to risk their lives any further.

"We cannot," said Breeza Meezy. "We're leaving them here. We will fly to the new cave in daylight while the owls are sleeping."

Carly thought sadly of all the little homes sitting empty. She was about to say something else when a loud whistle broke through the air. A rat came running from the cave entrance toward the tower.

"Your majesty," he said to Breeza Meezy when he reached them. "We must prepare for an attack — I was standing guard just now — they're coming from all directions!"

"The owls?" asked Breeza Meezy. "They won't be able to fly past the whistle root tree. We should be safe as long as we stay in the cave."

"No, your majesty," said the rat. "Not the owls. I

saw snakes, weasels, and foxes — more than I have ever seen before!"

"What? You mean they're all together?" asked Breeza Meezy in disbelief. "But they always hunt alone."

"Yes, your majesty, I don't understand it!"

"Get the other guards!" commanded Breeza Meezy. "Gather them in front of the cave! You must blow the whistle roots immediately. Go!"

The rat ran through the village banging on doors. Other rats emerged and followed him. There were eight of them altogether, and they ran toward the entrance of the cave carrying their whistle roots.

When they were outside, Carly heard one of them yell, "Now!" and the sudden blare of their whistles erupted like an explosion. The sound echoed through the cave, and Carly and the rats were thrown to the ground by the force of it. The houses and tower were shaking, and Carly feared they would break apart. Trying to block the sound was useless, but everyone had their hands over their ears. What else could they do? The terrible sound seemed to go on endlessly.

When it finally stopped, everything was quiet.

Carly didn't know if the attack was over or if she had gone deaf. But she soon heard voices coming from the front of the cave.

"They're still coming!"

The guard came running back to the tower.

"Your majesty," he said. "It didn't work!"

"Impossible!" said Breeza Meezy. "The whistle roots have always worked before!" But she was already thinking of a new plan. "We have to get every rat out of the cave. We'll fly away! It's sooner than planned but we don't have any choice."

"But your majesty," said the guard. "The night's

perfectly still. There aren't any breezes. There's no way for us to fly!"

"Is there another way out of the cave?" asked Carly.

"No," said Breeza Meezy. "There's not."

"I can help . . ." Carly pulled out the whistle roots that she kept around her neck. She hadn't been there to save Lewis, but she wasn't about to let more of the rats be taken — although she didn't feel as brave as she wished. "We'll make it even louder this time," she said.

Breeza Meezy agreed and Carly ran with the guard to the front of the cave.

The moon was in the sky. The other guards were standing in front of the whistle root tree and the creek was close by at their feet. And on the other side of the creek, the ground was alive with movement.

Animals were everywhere, growling and hissing, their eyes shining hungrily in the moonlight. They were closer than Carly had thought they would be, and snakes were beginning to swim across the creek. Carly looked around and saw foxes and weasels on top of the rock wall behind them, already climbing down toward the cave.

Animals were everywhere, growling and hissing,

their eyes shining hungrily in the moonlight.

"Now!" yelled one of the guards, and Carly raised the whistle roots to her mouth and blew into them as hard as she could.

The sound was worse than it had ever been. Carly was immediately dizzy from the pain in her head and ears. The ground seemed to shake and she was afraid she'd be knocked down again. But she forced herself to stay on her feet.

She kept blowing until there wasn't any air left in her lungs. And when she stopped, she realized that the rats had stopped blowing as well. They were staring in terror at the snakes that were crawling out of the creek in front of them.

The whistle roots hadn't worked.

"Get back in the cave!" she yelled to the rats. But as they turned to run, weasels entered the cave and several foxes stalked toward them. Carly and the rats backed up against the whistle root tree. There was no time to climb it. The animals would pounce on them as soon as they turned their backs.

Carly panicked as she imagined being bitten. Her mind raced with worry about what was happening to the rats still in the cave, especially Breeza Meezy.

"What's that sound?" one of the rats asked suddenly.

Carly listened. The animals were almost on them. The sound was faint, but it was growing stronger — it was bells!

She looked up at the whistle root tree and saw its leaves swinging back and forth. Was this really happening? But Carly also noticed that none of the other whistle root trees were moving; it was only the one in front of the rats' cave that was ringing.

And then it stopped, just as quickly as it had started.

"Look at the animals," a rat said.

Carly looked and saw that the animals seemed confused, as if they had woken up from a nap and found themselves surrounded by strangers.

She had an idea and lifted her whistle roots to her mouth and began to blow again. This time, the animals reacted immediately. They ran and slithered away to escape the sound, and plunged across the creek and into the woods beyond.

Carly ran into the cave, still blowing her whistle roots, and chased out every snake, weasel, and fox. She ran after them until they too were on the other side of the creek and she was certain they weren't coming back.

The attack was over and all of the rats in the cave

had survived. They had locked themselves in their houses, and Breeza Meezy had sealed herself in her tower.

"Begin preparations immediately," commanded Breeza Meezy when all of the rats had been accounted for. "We leave at sunrise. The Moon Child has saved us, but it's not safe to stay a moment longer."

Carly was about to explain that the whistle root tree had really saved them, but a rat spoke first asking, "How will we fly to the new cave if there aren't any breezes?"

"The breezes have already returned!" said another rat, who was standing near the cave entrance. Carly was standing there too, and she felt the breezes lifting her hair and twirling around her arms and legs, almost playfully.

Moonlight glowed on her pale skin. The rats gathered at her feet, gazing up at her and making her feel like a giant. They were whispering. Carly could hear them saying "Moon Child."

She looked out at the whistle root tree and saw that its leaves were moving again. Her heart raced for a second, but she quickly realized it was only the breezes causing it this time.

And when she looked up at the sky and saw the moon, she immediately thought of Lewis. She knew what he would be thinking if he were here.

Despite the attack, despite the whistle root tree ringing, despite the plans to leave in the morning, he would have thought what he always thought, no matter what the circumstances.

It was a perfect night for music.

CHAPTER THIRTEEN

NIGHT SOUNDS

his is from your uncle?" asked the substitute teacher when she looked at the note Green had handed her. He nodded. It was Monday morning and Carly's teacher, Ms. Hankel, wasn't there. Surprisingly though, Green was back in class.

"And your uncle's last name is Kunderskool?"

"Yes."

"But your last name's Pitcher . . . you don't have the same last name?"

"That happens sometimes with uncles."

The substitute stared at Green with a blank expression. "You know, I think I remember reading about you years ago in the newspaper. Wasn't your grandmother that crazy old woman who wouldn't leave her cabin when they wanted to build the school? What ever happened to her?"

"She died," said Green.

"Oh," the substitute said tactfully.

"May I go back to my desk?"

"Of course."

In her isolated corner of the room, Carly felt sick. Green's grandmother . . . dead? How could that have happened?

She tried to get Green's attention, but he never looked in her direction. First Lewis and now . . .

Carly felt her eyes closing and fought to keep them open. Not now! Green would think she didn't care. How could she fall asleep after hearing that his grandmother had died? She pinched herself, shook her arms, and looked up at the air-conditioning vent, hoping to get a blast of cold air in her face. But ultimately, there was nothing she could do.

Carly's head landed on her desk with a gentle, defeated thump.

"DOES SHE *ALWAYS* SLEEP LIKE this?" the substitute asked the class later that morning. She was clapping her hands and stomping her feet beside Carly's desk.

"Yes," said Hetta. "She must be the laziest person in Whistle Root."

"She is not," said Green. "She just can't sleep at night."

"Oh, yeah . . . and *that's* normal," Hetta replied.

When it was time for their study period, Green finally managed to wake Carly. And in the library, they chose a table away from the other students. They had just sat down when Hetta walked over.

"Well, well, well . . ." she said. "What *do* we have here? Looks like something green and bitter to me."

"Go away, Hetta," said Green.

"Green and Bitters. Makes me think of an unripe nut. And speaking of nuts, Green, what were you saying about your grandmother?"

"Stop it, Hetta!" said Carly. She looked anxiously at Green. How could Hetta be so cruel?

"Or maybe it makes me think of roots," continued Hetta. "Like the ones you're wearing around your neck, Bitters. Did you dig them out of the ground yourself? They look *lovely*."

Hetta laughed and walked away to join her friends at another table.

Carly touched her whistle roots self-consciously and tucked them back inside her shirt.

"Well, I like them," said Green. "Especially since I know they could blow Hetta's ears clear off her head."

Carly grinned. But her smile quickly faded and she told Green how sorry she was about his grandmother.

"What do you mean?" he asked.

"You told the substitute she died."

"Oh, well, most people think she died a long time ago," said Green. "And Granny likes to keep it that way."

"So she's not dead?" Carly felt relief sailing through her. "She's okay?"

"Well, she's still asleep, but she's not any worse. And I knew she'd be mad if I missed any more school, so . . . here I am."

"But what about the note from your uncle?"

Green smiled.

"I don't really have an uncle," he said. "Granny knew the school had to think I was living with someone, so she made him up." He suddenly thought of something. "Hey, why did you run away so fast the other night?"

Carly explained, and then told him everything that had happened since she'd last seen him.

"So that's what the kids were talking about," said Green.

"What do you mean?"

"Everyone was talking about the loud noise they heard coming from the woods last night. I think it even broke some windows. It must have been the whistle roots. I guess I couldn't hear it down in the cabin. You're really lucky you weren't hurt, you know. A lot of snakes in the woods are poisonous. And I sure wouldn't want to be bit by a weasel."

Green paused.

"I'm really sorry about Lewis," he said. "I wish I could have met him."

"All the other rats are gone now too," said Carly. "They left this morning for the new cave."

"Do you know where it is?"

"Not really. Breeza Meezy told me, but I'm not sure I could find it. And even if I could, I don't think I can walk there and back in one night. It's very far away."

How she would spend the lonely, wakeful nights that awaited her now that the rats were gone, Carly had no idea.

"It *must* have been the griddlebeast!" said Green with a scowl on his face. "What else could make the animals act like that? And what do you think made the whistle root tree ring? I thought they all had to ring together."

"Me too," replied Carly. "But I've been thinking about it. Maybe it was the whistle roots. Maybe if you blow enough of them, you can make a tree ring. Nothing like if there was a Crank and you turned it and all the trees were ringing. But maybe you can make one tree ring, for a little bit, in an emergency, like we did last night."

"We could test it!" said Green. "Tonight at the cave. I'll meet you there. We'll get a bunch of whistle roots and see if we can make it ring again."

"But what about your grandmother? She'll be alone in the cabin."

"She's alone right now," said Green. "There's really nothing I can do for her when I'm there. But if this works, then maybe we could help her. We could get her out of the cabin and near a whistle root tree and make it ring. Maybe that would break whatever spell the griddlebeast put on her."

THAT NIGHT, CARLY WAITED FOR Green outside the cave, which she had told him how to find. She was nervous. She had realized it was a mistake for them to meet here. The griddlebeast knew where the cave was. What if it sent the animals back for another attack? Or what if it snuck up on Carly and Green with its whispers? If the griddlebeast put Green to sleep, Carly wouldn't be able to blow enough whistle roots by herself to make the tree ring. And she didn't think she was strong enough to carry Green all the way back to the cabin. What would she do then?

An owl flew by and startled Carly. But the owl didn't stop and silently disappeared into the darkness of the woods.

"Stupid owl," said Carly, and then felt bad because she knew Breeza Meezy and Lewis would have been upset with her for saying it.

She sat down and was about to snap off some whistle roots for Green when she heard something. It was faint and sounded as if it was coming from very far away.

"What's that?" she said softly.

"What's what?" a voice in the darkness replied.

Carly jumped to her feet, lifting her whistle roots to her mouth so fast they knocked against her teeth.

"Whoa, hey, it's just me." Green jumped over the creek. "Sorry about that. I didn't mean to scare you. What were you doing?"

"I heard something," said Carly, lowering the whistle roots.

"Was it me?" asked Green. "I tried to walk quietly but it's hard to do in the dark. I must have tripped fifty times on my way here, mainly on whistle roots."

"No, I don't think it was you," said Carly. "Listen, do you hear anything?"

Green was quiet and listened to the sounds of the woods at night.

"I don't really know what I'm listening for," he said. "But I don't think I hear it."

"I don't hear it anymore either."

"What was it?"

"I don't know. I mean it could have been . . . let's just forget it. Are you ready?"

"Before we do that, could I take a look in the cave?" asked Green. "I've been dying to see it."

Carly hesitated because she didn't want them staying any longer than necessary. But then she agreed and took Green around the whistle root tree and into the cave. She handed him her flashlight since he didn't seem to have one.

"Wow," said Green, as he swept the light over the abandoned little houses. "This is amazing. It's just like you described it." He walked slowly through the village, admiring the whimsically carved windows and the artful chimneys made of small stones, snail shells, and mortar; one even twisted into the air like a cat's tail.

Carly stood at the entrance and felt as though she was looking at a ghost town, or maybe a display of empty dollhouses in a toy store. Until she'd actually seen it, she'd been able to imagine that the rats were still there, tending their fires and going about their lives as they normally did.

But now she knew — the rats were really gone.

Once they were back outside, Green pulled some cotton balls out of his pocket. "I thought we could use these," he said. "No sense in us going deaf." He had also brought some whistle roots because he hadn't thought it wise to walk through the woods without them. They had thirteen whistle roots between them, the exact number Carly and the rats had used the night before.

"Ready?" asked Carly, after they had stuffed the cotton in their ears.

Green nodded.

They began to blow and the sound was again shockingly loud. It was only slightly muffled by the cotton. Carly looked at Green and could tell he was feeling the same pain that she was. But he didn't stop, and they both watched the leaves of the whistle root tree.

There wasn't any movement.

Carly snapped off another whistle root to bring the total to fourteen, but still nothing happened.

"Should we try again?" asked Green, struggling to get air back into his lungs when they had finally stopped blowing.

"I don't think it's going to work," said Carly, disappointed and also breathing hard. "Something else must have made the tree ring last night."

"Like what?"

"I don't know. But I think we need to get out of here." The griddlebeast would have surely heard the noise they made. "C'mon, I want to check something anyway."

Carly led Green through the woods toward the white cradle. When they reached it, she lifted the red hat and looked inside.

"Is there a new message?" asked Green, who was holding the flashlight. He hadn't seen the hat before, but Carly had told him about it. He studied the hat just as closely as he had the houses in the rats' cave.

"No, it's just the note I left the other night." Carly stared at what she'd written and suddenly realized something: Maybe her note was too long. The notes she'd found in the hat had always been so short. She asked Green if he had something to write with. He pulled a short pencil out of his shirt pocket and handed it to her.

Carly tore a strip of paper from her original note and wrote a single sentence:

How do we make the whistle root trees ring if there is no Crank?

She put the note in the hat and then put the hat back in the cradle. They immediately heard a sound like a single kernel of corn popping. She lifted the hat; her note was gone.

Carly and Green waited, not knowing what to do. Then they heard the popping sound again. Carly still had the hat in her hands and when she looked down, there was a new note inside. She grabbed it and she and Green read it together:

WHEREVER THERE ARE WHISTLE
ROOT TREES THERE IS
ALWAYS A CRANK.

They looked at each other in astonishment. Carly tore off another strip of paper and wrote another note:

Well, where is it?

"Isn't that a bit rude?" asked Green.

Carly and Green read the note together.

Carly shrugged. She was tired of the hat never telling her exactly what she needed to know. She put the note in the hat, and the hat in the cradle, and they heard the same popping sound. Then they waited again. They waited for almost an hour. Carly kept lifting the hat to check it, but this time, they didn't receive any response.

"Well, at least we know there's a Crank," said Green, trying not to yawn. It was very late, which of course wasn't a problem for Carly. But Green still had to walk back to the cabin and get at least some sleep before waking up for school.

Carly went part of the way with him. Then she checked that he had his whistle roots and made him promise to blow them if he heard the faintest hint of a whisper. Still, she worried as he walked off through the dark woods.

She didn't want to lose another friend.

Walking home by herself, Carly noticed how lonely and threatening the woods felt with the rats gone. She was thinking about how much she missed them when she heard the same sound she had heard earlier at the cave. It still sounded far away, and she couldn't tell which direction it was coming from. She strained her ears to hear it more clearly.

Breezes rustled the leaves in the trees and insects chirped and whirred. The sound was so faint that Carly kept losing track of it, but she was always able to find it again. And all of a sudden, she realized what it was.

It was the sound of a fiddle.

CHAPTER FOURTEEN

SOMETHING IN
THE CHIMNEY

he griddlebeast had always planned to chop down the whistle root trees. Not with his own spindly hands, of course. His whispers would take care of it, when the time came. He should have done it before now, he knew, but there had been so many distractions! Aside from whispering to the owls, the creek, and Granny Pitcher, there had been all of those delicious rabbits to eat! And his beautiful feathers — he was constantly losing them and having to intrude upon the owls in their tree holes to steal more.

But the ringing whistle root tree at the rats' cave had changed everything.

It had been such a difficult attack to plan. He had whispered to every snake, weasel, and fox in the woods and beyond. He had even set up a fire near the rats' cave to catch the breezes. Breezes loved to play with smoke; he knew that from watching them around the dead whistle root tree at his burrow. And when the breezes flew in to play with the smoke at his fire, he whispered that they should avoid the rats' cave. And they had, as far as he could tell, for he watched everything and none of the rats had been able to fly away.

But then the whistle root tree had rung and the spell of his whispers had been broken. He hadn't known that anything could do that. He was at least glad to find it hadn't affected all of his whispers. The owls were still flying off with rats, although not the rats he wanted them to catch — just regular rats. The other rats, the ones who lived in the cave, had flown away the next morning, and he knew he would have to search for them soon.

But still, it worried him that the whistle root trees could ring unexpectedly and break his whispers. And so the next night, while Carly and Green were waiting for messages from the red hat, he had crawled down every chimney in the town of Whistle Root, sat on every pillow next to every sleeping head, and whispered the same words to each of them: "Chop down the whistle root trees."

He didn't lose any owl feathers in the beds he visited that night. For, oddly enough, when he heard the whistle root tree ring, the quills had pierced his skin. It had hurt just for a moment. And then, it was as if the feathers had been part of him all along, and not merely stolen from the sleeping owls.

He couldn't help admiring himself in the mirrors of the houses he entered.

A small child woke up while he was looking at his feathers and asked him who he was. The griddlebeast just laughed, and the child screamed when she heard the terrible griddles coming from his mouth.

He leaped onto her bed and whispered, "Chop down the whistle root trees." Then, tired of her screaming, he hopped out her bedroom door, pretending to be a rabbit. But she apparently didn't like rabbits, because she kept screaming, and the griddlebeast clambered back up the chimney onto the roof to escape the sound. There, he spread his arms wide, ready to fly into the night — but he didn't go anywhere. For although he had feathers, he couldn't fly, and had to settle for scrambling down some vines that grew up one side of the house.

He knew the rats flew on breezes, but he didn't know how. He tried whispering to the breezes, ordering them to carry him, but they had only been able to drag him painfully over the ground, which wasn't like flying at all. Even though he wasn't very big, he was bigger than a rat, and he assumed that was the problem.

He ran into the woods on all fours on his way to the next house. The woods, he thought happily, would soon be gone forever.

"Very busy tonight," he called to a small group of rabbits as he ran hurriedly past. They were sitting in the moonlight and it had seemed polite to explain why he hadn't stopped to eat them.

CHAPTER FIFTEEN

The Axe Thief

he next morning, there was no school in Whistle Root.

It is Tuesday, isn't it? Carly asked herself as she peered through the windows of the locked building. The halls were empty and the lights were off. She didn't see a single teacher or student. She tried the front doors but they were locked, so she walked to the cafeteria and tried the door she had used on Saturday night; it was still open. She slipped inside and made her way through the empty halls to the library, and down the ladder to the cabin.

"Where is everybody?" she asked Green when he lifted the wood board from the fireplace.

"I don't know," he said. "I was up there earlier and couldn't find anyone. It's not a holiday, is it?"

"I don't think so," said Carly. "Unless they made

an announcement on Friday that we missed. But you'd think they would have announced it again yesterday."

"Maybe the substitute forgot," said Green. "But look over here — I grabbed as many books as I could from the library this morning. Want to go through them with me?"

Carly looked toward the corner where Green kept the books and immediately noticed that something was missing.

"Where's Elzick?" she asked.

"Oh, I tripped the other night and fell and knocked him off his perch. He's around here somewhere."

They both sat down and started looking through the books, but Carly's eyes were already closing. She had sat at her window the rest of the night listening to the sound of the fiddle, trying to figure out where it was coming from. She desperately wanted it to be Lewis, but how could he still be alive? None of the other musicians had survived the owl attacks. And a part of her mind couldn't help thinking about the stories of the King of Endroot wandering through the forest playing his fiddle. She knew it wasn't likely, or really even possible, but what if the Moon King . . .

"Carly," said Green. "Why don't you lie down on the couch and sleep. I'll get something from the garden later and wake you for lunch."

Carly was so tired, she knew it was pointless to refuse. She walked to the couch and was asleep within seconds.

WHEN CARLY WOKE UP, GREEN was gone. She had no idea how long she'd been asleep. It was impossible to tell the time of day down in the cabin.

In the dim light of the lanterns, she saw Green's grandmother sleeping in the bed. She also saw Elzick's empty perch and wished she knew exactly where he was. She knew it was silly — he *was* stuffed, after all — but she couldn't help fearing he was about to swoop out of some dark corner (of which there were many in the cabin) and attack her.

She went to the front door, opened it cautiously, and looked out into the tunnel. "Green?" she called, but there was no answer. She remembered he'd said he was going to the garden. And not wanting to stay in the cabin by herself, she grabbed a candle and set out after him.

When she finally reached the end of the tunnel, she

found Green, lying at
the foot of the ladder.

He was asleep just like his
grandmother.

Carly dropped to the ground beside him and shook his shoulder. She
said his name again and again, but knew
it wasn't any use.

She hadn't been there to protect
Lewis when the owls took him. And
now she had failed Green because
she was sleeping, like always. She
could've helped him if she'd been
there, blown her whistle roots,
maybe have scared the griddlebeast off. What if Green was
asleep forever now?

"I'll find the Crank," she told
him, trying not to cry. "Don't
worry, Green . . . I'll find
it . . . I'll make
the whistle root

trees ring . . ." She knew the ringing whistle root tree at the rats' cave hadn't woken Green's grandmother. But that had been only one tree, and it wasn't near the cabin. Surely if she could make them all ring . . .

She looked up at the door and saw darkness through the keyhole. It was night again — the griddlebeast wouldn't be able to make her sleep.

Finding Green's key, she climbed up the ladder and emerged into the light of the moon.

CARLY KNEW IMMEDIATELY THAT something was terribly wrong in the woods.

She rushed toward firelight, toward sounds that sickened her. A group of people from the town were crowded around a whistle root tree. They all had axes and were chopping at the massive old trunk.

To Carly's horror, she saw that several of the ancient trees had already fallen.

They can't! thought Carly. *If they chop down the whistle root trees . . .*

Without hesitating, she pulled out her whistle roots and blew them at the townspeople, many of whom dropped their axes right away to cover their ears. Others simply stood there, dumbfounded at

They were chopping at the massive old trunk.

finding themselves under attack by a small girl with what appeared to be a pan flute.

Gathering as many of the dropped axes as she could carry, Carly ran off and hid them in the rats' cave. She didn't know where else to put them. And she hoped the griddlebeast wasn't watching the cave as closely now that the rats were gone.

Then she ran back into the woods, blowing her whistle roots at everyone she found.

By morning, Carly had a cave full of axes and an angry mob looking for her. She didn't think it was safe to go home. And she knew she had to get out of the woods before the sun rose. She couldn't risk falling asleep outside. She wanted to go back to the tunnel and see Green but feared she wouldn't get there in time — the sky was already growing lighter.

She would have to sleep in the cave; it was her only option.

But before she did, she checked the red hat, which was nearby after all, and found a new note in it that said:

Lew Kunderskool

A name? she thought irritably. It was giving her a name? What help was that? Why wouldn't it tell her where the Crank was?

But then she realized she had heard the last name before. It was Green's uncle's last name, wasn't it? Was the note telling her to find him? Was his first name Lew? Green had never said.

But then she remembered Green didn't really have an uncle. His grandmother had made him up because the school had to think he was living with *someone* and everyone thought *she* was dead.

Before she could think about it more, the first rays of sunlight burst through the trees and Carly knew she had to get back to the cave fast.

She turned to run, but had taken only a few steps when she heard the whisper. "Sleep . . ." the whisper said, just as it had at the smoking whistle root tree so many nights before.

Carly spun around, looking for the griddlebeast, but her eyes were already closing. It was morning. She had been caught outside in sunlight.

The last thing she heard before falling into a terrified sleep was the sound of griddles echoing through the air around her.

CHAPTER SIXTEEN

THE WOOP OF THE WITTERY

hen Carly woke up, she saw fire, rocks, and feathers — exactly what Lewis had described when they'd gone to the smoking whistle root tree.

She was in the griddlebeast's burrow.

Her hand went immediately to her neck, but the whistle roots were gone. She was lying on the ground and knew she wouldn't be able to stand up — there wasn't enough room. She would have to crawl out of the burrow. But before she could move, she realized that she wasn't alone.

"I believe you have my hat," a voice said.

Carly looked around and saw a little man standing beside the fire. He was only about a foot tall and had a red marching band hat on his head — just like the one from the cradle. The only difference was that his had a large feather stuck in the top of it. He wore gray pants tucked into long black boots and a dark blue jacket with brassy buttons on the front and tails in the back. His shaggy white mustache and goatee made him look very old. In fact, everything about him looked worn and tattered. The epaulet on one shoulder had even been replaced with a crab.

"Who are you?" asked Carly, although she had already begun to guess. "Are you the one who sent the notes?"

"Of course," said the man. "The rats put a white cradle in the woods, didn't they?"

"Well, yes," said Carly. "But that's because they have this old saying, 'A white cradle in the woods brings hope' and —"

"The saying is actually, 'A white cradle in the woods brings Woop,'" said the man, interrupting Carly. "I knew I should have written it down for them . . . but they couldn't read . . . I really should have taught them how to read. Excuse me for a moment, won't you?" He pulled a telescope from his pocket and stared through it toward nothing in particular that Carly could see. "Oh, for goodness sake!" he said, and put the telescope back in his pocket.

"What were you looking at?" asked Carly.

"Someone put a clock in a cabbage patch," the man said bitterly.

"You saw that from here?"

"Not very well ... my telescope is easily distracted." The man began dusting his uniform with his hands. "Haven't been in a rabbit burrow in years," he said, and immediately fell asleep — while still standing.

The crab, which Carly had assumed was dead, suddenly jumped to life and pinched the man on the ear. It then went back to being an epaulet.

"Thank you, Crustace," said the man, wincing and opening his eyes. He then unscrewed the cap from his canteen and poured a little water on his shoulder. "Reminds him of the ocean," he said to Carly, who had begun to think she was still dreaming.

"Who are you?" she asked again, since she hadn't really gotten an answer.

"I'm the Woop of the Wittery," said the man. "And I've traveled far to be here tonight. Oh, excuse me

"Oh, the impatience!"

again, will you?" He pulled his telescope back out and looked in a completely different direction. "Oh, the impatience!" he exclaimed. "If they put one more spoon in that spider web, I may not answer them at all."

"What do you keep looking at?" asked Carly, although she had already decided that the little man was completely mad.

"Trifling, trifling," said the man. "It's always something trifling. Why do they bother me with trifles?"

"Who?" asked Carly. "Who's bothering you?"

"Everyone!" said the man plaintively. "Everyone I've ever helped."

"Did you ever help the rats?" asked Carly, remembering what he had said about teaching them to read.

"Of course," said the man. "I taught them to speak and I taught them to fly. Though if I hadn't, I'd probably be back at the Wittery enjoying a nice trout supper right now. But Crassifolia was always wanting —" There was a sudden popping sound and the man jumped and swore and swatted at his ear as if something had stung him. A small piece of white paper fluttered out from under his hat and landed on the ground in front of him. He snatched it up, read it, and tore it into tiny pieces while grumbling angrily to himself. He then yanked the feather out of his hat and scribbled something on a piece of paper that the crab had pulled from his pocket and handed to him. When finished, he tucked the note up into his hat and there was another popping sound and the man jumped as if having gotten a shock. He then poured more water on his shoulder and continued exactly where he had left off. "— favors for the young king and I did feel sorry for him. So I traveled to the Endroot and taught the rats to speak like she asked and —"

"Do you mean the Moon King?" asked Carly, interrupting him. But even that was only one of a hundred questions she wanted to ask.

"Yes, of course," said the man. "That's what the guards called him. And then the rats began calling him that too. But they did it *respectfully*, whereas the guards were just cruel. They wouldn't let any- one visit him. The rats were the only creatures able to reach him in the dungeon. And Crassifolia thought they could carry messages to him — and they did — but they also befriended the young king. And he, clever boy that he was, taught them to play the instruments his family had been playing for centuries — the fiddle, the horn, and the drum — which spooked the guards unendingly because they could never figure out where the music was coming from. The boy made the little instruments himself, of course, and sent the rats to gather whatever materials he needed. I even have a drum he made sitting beside my bed at the Wittery. I used to play it whenever I couldn't sleep. But I never sleep now — my hat and telescope won't let me — and if I do fall asleep, I've taught Crustace here to wake me so they don't get the pleasure."

He patted the crab affectionately and then pulled his telescope back out and looked in another direction entirely.

"You said you taught them to fly," said Carly. "Did Crassifolia ask you to do that too?"

"Oh, no," said the man, putting his telescope away and scribbling angrily on another note. "That was the boy's plan. He asked me to create an army of flying rats

— and I did — though it took time. I taught them to speak and fly, and he taught them to play music. Not all of the rats could learn to play, mind you, but many of them could. And when he had enough, he unleashed them on the Kingdom of Endroot like a plague."

A strong gust of wind rushed into the burrow, roaring powerfully and circling Carly and the man.

"Not yet, my old friend!" said the man loudly. "Please wait outside! We don't want to lose the fire!" The wind rushed back out and the man tucked the note he had written up into his hat and jumped again when the popping sound came. He then continued his story. "The rats played their music endlessly, on every roof of every house that had been built since the whistle root trees were chopped down. And they played all over the castle too, tormenting the king, who was the boy's oldest brother. And when anyone tried to catch them, they just flew away on the breezes as I'd taught them to do. This went on for weeks and no one in the kingdom could sleep. And then the boy told the king that he could get rid of the rats if he was allowed to leave the dungeon.

"The king was desperate by that point — and only

half awake — and agreed to release his brother. And so, the boy walked out into the moonlight for the first time in three years. He immediately called for his father's fiddle and played it as he traveled through the kingdom gathering the rats to him."

The man abruptly pulled his telescope out again and looked directly at Carly.

"Stop showing me that!" he said, and struggled with his telescope to get it back into his pocket. "I've already given it to her!"

"Were you looking at me?" asked Carly.

"No," said the man. "The telescope was showing me that name again."

"What name?"

"The one I sent you," said the man. "Didn't you get the last note?"

"I did," said Carly. "But what did it mean? It was just the name of a man. I don't think he even exists."

"How should I know what it means?" asked the man angrily.

"You sent the note, didn't you?"

"I can't control what the telescope shows me. I just know when it wants to show me something."

"Has it shown you where the Crank is?"

"No."

"But you're sure there is one, right? Your note said —"

"I know what I wrote," the man interrupted. "And wherever there are whistle root trees, there is always a Crank, and always only one. It has to be in these woods somewhere. And turning it is the only way to stop the griddlebeast, which is why I've come."

"You're going to help me find it?" said Carly. "Oh, thank you! I didn't know where to look and there's no time to waste because —"

"Oh, I didn't come to find the Crank," said the man. "I came to get my hat back. I think you're lying on it."

Carly felt around with her hand and found the hat from the cradle crushed beneath her. She remembered she'd been holding it when the griddlebeast whispered her to sleep.

"You could have taken better care of it," said the man disapprovingly. "I have so few of them left. But I suppose its condition won't matter much in the cabbage patch."

"You're sending it to a cabbage patch?"

"They put a clock in it, didn't they? Just like you

and the rats put a white cradle in the woods. I tell everyone something different — it just has to be unique so I know who's calling me. And someone is *always* calling me, which is why I rarely travel anymore. I'm too busy at the Wittery. Speaking of which, I should be getting back, so if you'd just give me the hat —"

"Wait," said Carly. "You have to help me!"

"I've helped you all I can," said the man. "And I don't know where the Crank is, so there's nothing more I can do. Though it is a shame the whistle root trees will be gone soon — *again* — just like in the Endroot. It certainly is odd how people are always chopping them down. They're lovely trees really."

"Is there another way to make them ring?" asked Carly. "Without the Crank, I mean. One did, a few nights ago, but I don't know how it —"

"Someone must have turned the Crank," said the man with certainty. "There is no other way to make them ring. And if only one rang, then the Crank must have been turned only a little. The oldest trees ring first, you see. I wonder why they didn't turn it more?"

"Could it have been the Moon King?" asked Carly, knowing the question might be foolish. "I've heard fiddle music — in the woods — and the rats have all left or been taken by the owls."

"Impossible," said the man. "He's been gone a very long time, my dear. And I'm afraid these woods will soon be gone as well, unless you find the Crank, of course. And I am sorry, but I really must go. So if you'd please give me the hat, I'll be on my way."

Carly didn't want to give the hat back, but it seemed childish to refuse. She straightened it out as best she could and handed it to the man.

"What happened after the Moon King had gathered all the rats?" she asked. He could at least finish the story for her, and maybe there would be some clue that would help her find the Crank.

"Well," said the man, inspecting the still crumpled hat, "he marched them into what little remained of the forest and was never seen in the Endroot again."

"Is that when he came here?"

"Yes. Crassifolia helped him, although it still took almost a year of traveling. And she gave him a bag of seeds, just like the one she'd given his father. But it wasn't a mixed bag of seeds like his father's had been — the one she gave the Moon King had only the seeds of whistle root trees in it."

"Why?"

"She wanted to give him the strongest protection possible. And he planted them in an empty land, much like the Endroot had been, although the ground wasn't made of ash. And on moonlit nights, he wandered among the young whistle root trees playing his father's fiddle to help them grow, for the trees needed moonlight and music even more than the sun. And the rats helped him and began to play only in moonlight as well. And they played only in groups of three — one for the fiddle, one for the horn, and one for the drum — just as the Moon King's family had always done. And when the trees grew tall, the Moon King told the rats to play up high so that they'd be safe from the animals that had moved into the new woods and were a danger to them. But even up high, they still had to worry about the owls, so the Moon King asked for my help again. And I traveled here and taught the owls to enjoy the rats' music and even to dance when they heard them playing. But that was a long time ago. I don't know any of the rats living here today, and I haven't been back to these woods until tonight."

"And what about the vegetables?" asked Carly.

"Why do the rats always replace a lost band member with a vegetable?"

"Oh," said the man, looking a bit sheepish. "They still do that, do they? Well, that was a bit of foolishness on my part. It's funny how a whim becomes a law, isn't it? Or is that scary? I forget which."

He suddenly pulled his telescope out again and stared toward the tunnel leading out of the burrow.

"The griddlebeast's coming back — he'll be here soon," he said, and then jumped and swore and swatted at his ear as another small piece of paper fluttered to the ground. "Oh, *really!*" he said irritably, as he picked it up and handed it to Crustace. "I won't answer it till Christmas!" The wind blew back into the burrow and the man reached out and moved his fingers up and down as if playing a piano. "Tisk, tisk, tisk," he said, and then he was flying, almost bumping into Carly. "Down the tunnel, my friend!" he called, and the wind rushed out of the burrow, pulling the man by his arm like a child being dragged to bed.

"WAIT, TAKE ME WITH YOU!" yelled Carly. Then she remembered her own experience with the wind and how it had fought her every attempt to steer it. "YOU CAN CONTROL THE WIND?"

"THIS IS THE ONLY GUST I TRUST!" the man yelled back.

And then he was gone.

CHAPTER SEVENTEEN

THE OLD OWL
AND THE WHIRLWIND

arly stared after the man for less than a second and then crawled frantically out of the burrow, squeezing her way down the tunnel. As soon as she was outside, she took off running. She didn't even stop to look back at the smoking whistle root tree.

It was night again. That must be why she had woken up. Carly wondered if the griddlebeast had thought she wouldn't.

She ran away from the sounds of axes chopping down trees. She was constantly afraid she would hear whispers — but instead, after several minutes had gone by, she heard howling. It came from the direction of the burrow and she knew the griddlebeast had discovered she was gone, which made her run even faster.

She ran for a long time and was soon deeper in the woods than she had ever been before. When she couldn't run anymore, she stopped briefly to rest. She wondered if the griddlebeast was following her and listened for noises that might let her know. Instead of footsteps, she heard the sound of a fiddle, and quickly but quietly crept toward it.

And when she finally saw who was playing it, she cried out, "Lewis! Lewis!" and ran toward him.

Although Lewis saw her, he didn't stop playing his fiddle, which wasn't all that odd since he never wanted to stop playing. But he was also playing on the ground and by himself, which certainly *was* odd.

He acknowledged Carly with a grin and then nodded his head toward something a little farther away. Carly stopped and looked and saw a large old owl hopping from foot to foot on top of a small dead tree. The owl was only about ten feet away and was watching Lewis intently. And whenever there was a pause in the music, it lifted its wings and lowered its head as if preparing to fly directly at him.

Lewis changed songs abruptly from the fast one he was playing to a slow one that reminded Carly of a lullaby. She watched as the owl closed its eyes and tucked its head lower within its feathers. And when the song was over, the owl seemed completely asleep.

"What are you doing here?" Lewis whispered to Carly.

"I heard you playing," Carly whispered back. "Well, I didn't *know* it was you. I thought you were dead. Oh, Lewis, I found the squash and the onion on my roof and thought the owls had gotten you."

"They did," whispered Lewis. "Or at least one did — this one. He took me when I stopped playing for a moment to tune my strings."

Carly looked over at the owl to make sure he was still sleeping.

"He's probably the oldest one in the woods," whispered Lewis. "He's listened to me play since my first night on a roof."

"But how come he's listening to you play *now?*" asked Carly. "I thought all the owls had stopped doing that."

"He must still appreciate good music," said Lewis. "Though he is a bit deaf. But I've been playing loudly and that's probably why he hasn't eaten me yet."

"But couldn't you have gotten away?" asked Carly. "Like now — when he's asleep? You could have just played him a lullaby and then flown back to the cave on a breeze. What are you still doing here?"

Lewis hesitated.

"Well, I did plan to go back," he whispered. "But he's not a bad audience really, aside from trying to eat me whenever I stop playing. And out here, I haven't had to worry about vegetables or the other rules. Though I do hate to think what will happen if Breeza Meezy finds out. Say, did you bring your horn?"

"No," whispered Carly. "And you shouldn't play your fiddle any more, either. Listen, that creature I saw at the smoking whistle root tree —"

"Not play?"

"— is called a griddlebeast and may be following me — I

don't know for sure, but we shouldn't make any more noise —"

Something large hit the side of Carly's head and almost knocked her to the ground. The sudden sound of Lewis's fiddle erupted into the night. He was playing a fast and wild song, and Carly looked up to see the old owl flying back to the dead tree. He had woken up and flown silently at them while they were talking. But as Lewis continued to play, the owl settled back on his perch and soon began hopping from foot to foot as if nothing had happened.

Carly wasn't hurt. And oddly, the name from the last note in the red hat had begun circling in her head insistently. It seemed to beat a perfect rhythm with the song Lewis was playing — Lew *Kunderskool*, Lew *Kunderskool*, Lew *Kunderskool*.

She wanted to tell Lewis to play slow again so that the owl would go back to sleep. She also wanted the name to stop repeating so that she could think and figure out what to do next. But when Lewis began to play even faster, the name circled faster too. And as the sounds all merged together, she finally realized what it meant.

Lew *Kun*derskool, Lew*Kun*derskool, lewkunder-skool, lookunderschool.

"Look under school!" she said aloud, and gasped. Green's cabin!

Her mind began to race and she looked toward the old owl on the small dead tree and felt like gasping again. The Crank had been there all along and she had never even realized it.

She had to get back to the cabin as quickly as possible.

She glanced at Lewis, who was still playing his fiddle and hadn't been listening to her at all.

"There's another owl," he said over his music, and nodded toward the branches of a nearby whistle root tree.

Carly didn't want to look. Her instincts told her it wasn't an owl Lewis had seen, despite the feathers. And when she finally raised her eyes, she saw what she had feared most.

The griddlebeast had found them.

CARLY'S HAND JUMPED TO HER neck, but she hadn't had time to get new whistle roots. She had to do something — she couldn't let the griddlebeast whisper Lewis to sleep.

"Play louder!" she said, hoping the griddlebeast's whispers wouldn't work if they couldn't hear them. She figured that was why the deaf old owl hadn't eaten Lewis yet — he hadn't been able to hear the whispers as well as the other owls had.

"The new fellow's a bit odd," said Lewis.

"It's not an owl!" said Carly urgently. "It's the griddlebeast! That's what I was trying to tell you. He's behind everything — the owls taking the rats, the creek rising, the whistle root trees being chopped down —"

"Someone's chopping down the whistle root trees?"

"Yes! The whole town is! And he does it all with whispers, so you've got to play louder so we can't hear him!"

Carly wanted to tell Lewis to fly away to safety, but there weren't any breezes. The night was very still. A full moon was shining through the leaves of the whistle root trees. In its light, Carly watched as the griddlebeast jumped from the branch he'd been sitting on. He landed on the ground without making a sound and combed his fingers through his feathers, which had been ruffled by the fall.

He then began to walk toward them. And he was whispering.

Carly was about to grab Lewis and run when the wind began to blow fiercely. Or rather, the wind began to blow fiercely around Carly. She was engulfed in a whirlwind while everything just a few feet away remained perfectly still. Her hair and clothes whipped around wildly, making it look as if a sudden new power was surging through her. But she knew the griddlebeast had done it and feared she would be trapped forever by the invisible whirling walls, or carried away and dropped somewhere to die, like the middle of a desert or ocean.

She also noticed,

however, that
the griddlebeast
had stopped walking and was star-
ing at her with a surprised look on his face. And then
her hands began to jump up and down as if she were
a marionette and someone was pulling the strings.
Only they weren't being pulled from above, they were
being bumped from below — by the wind — over
and over again. And when the next bump hit her right
hand, she pushed down with her fingers and found
the tisks and was immediately lifted upward. She let
go and dropped back to the ground and the wind continued to bump her hands, ever more insistently.

The griddlebeast hadn't caused the whirlwind
after all.

"I think it's from
the Woop!" Carly shouted to Lewis.

With no time to explain, and hoping she was right, Carly reached through the wall of wind with her left hand and grabbed Lewis. She then found the tisks again with her right hand and flew up into the night.

"We have to get to the school!" she yelled to Lewis, who didn't look at all pleased about being grabbed. But he had seen the griddlebeast running toward them and didn't protest as much as he normally might.

"We won't be able to control the wind!" he said. He reached out with his toes anyway and found several tisks, and Carly opened her hand to release him.

They were flying straight up toward the stars.

"Press down!" yelled Carly, which she and Lewis did, and the wind curved back down toward the trees.

"Look out!" The old owl was flying at them and they swerved, barely avoiding a collision.

Easily outdistancing the old owl, Carly took charge of the gust of wind and turned it abruptly in the direction in which she wanted to go. The gust obeyed her immediately.

"How are you doing that so easily?" asked Lewis, clearly impressed with her mastery of the wind.

"I'll tell you later!" said Carly. The woods passed under them in a moonlit blur. It was wondrous, flying so fast through the night sky, but there wasn't time to enjoy it. Carly scanned the tops of the trees, looking for . . .

She suddenly dive-bombed into a small clearing. When she got close to the ground, she let go of the tisks, grabbed Lewis, and dropped several feet into the garden hidden below them. She rolled noisily through the untidy rows of plants and finally came to a stop with a pumpkin squashed beneath her.

The wind was gone. And there wasn't any sign of the griddlebeast — at least for the moment.

She ran to the door that hid the tunnel to the cabin. She fumbled for the key but couldn't find it, and began jumping up and down on the door. She felt the old rotten wood beginning to give way. It collapsed suddenly, and she fell down into the tunnel.

Moonlight streamed down with her. And once she had wiped the dirt and debris from her eyes, she saw that she had almost landed on top of Green.

"Who's that?" asked Lewis, as he flew down shakily on a weak breeze he'd found.

"A friend," said Carly. She had to get to the cabin as quickly as possible and knew she couldn't pull or carry Green. "Please stay with him, Lewis. And if you see the griddlebeast, play as loudly as you can!"

Before Lewis could say anything, she took off running down the tunnel. She didn't have any light. She held her hands out in front of her and raced through the darkness. She tripped and fell several times, but always got up and kept running. She tried not to scream when unseen roots brushed against her face, arms, and legs. She tried to remember that most of them were from whistle root trees, which made it only slightly less terrifying.

Without warning, she crashed into the door of the cabin, knocking it open. It was completely dark inside, and she felt her way toward the corner where Elzick's perch was. When she found it, she felt quickly for the top, fearing all the while that Elzick would be sitting there. But he wasn't. So she took a deep breath and began to turn the Crank.

It wouldn't move at first and Carly panicked, thinking she'd been wrong. But then it began to creak and groan. And once she got it moving, it turned easily, spinning round and round. She had no intention of stopping. But then someone lit a candle, and Carly looked up and saw that Green's grandmother had gotten out of bed.

"That should be enough, dear," Granny Pitcher said, smiling and pulling on her well-worn cloak and boots.

She began to turn the Crank.

CHAPTER EIGHTEEN

A BAG OF SEEDS

arly and Granny Pitcher found Green at the top of the ladder, awake and staring into the woods.

"It was just like the story described it," he said excitedly, hugging his grandmother and listening to Lewis ask him if he knew how to play the drum.

The leaves had stopped moving, but the echo of a million bells was still in the air. The four of them stood in the clearing, aglow with moonlight, and listened as the ringing faded away. Granny Pitcher had an arm around both Carly and Green. She even invited Lewis to sit on her shoulder.

When it was silent, Carly told them everything that had happened while they'd been asleep. She had to go back further for Granny Pitcher's sake, but concluded with the chopping of the whistle root trees, the Woop, and how she had known where the Crank was.

"I remembered what Green had said about bumping into Elzick's perch. I realized that must have been on the night when the whistle root tree at the cave rang."

Granny Pitcher asked lots of questions about the griddlebeast. While Carly and Green answered, she searched the woods with her eyes as if trying to find it. She seemed particularly interested when they mentioned its feathers. "I wonder . . ." she began, but didn't say anything more.

"Did you know Elzick's perch was the Crank?" Green asked her.

"Of course," she said. "That's why I built the cabin around it — so no one else would find it. But Carly luckily figured out the one clue I left — a name — and I'm very grateful for her cleverness." She smiled at Carly and then pulled the hood from her cloak up over her head. "I know you two have lots of questions, but there's something I must do. I promise to explain everything when I get back." She then disappeared so quickly into the darkness of the woods that there was no hope of following her.

TWO DAYS LATER, MOST PEOPLE in Whistle Root were denying they had heard bells ringing or that they had seen the leaves of the whistle root trees swinging back and forth. It was harder to explain why they had suddenly decided to chop down the whis- tle root trees. You couldn't deny that — stumps were everywhere.

Back in school, teachers and students looked away when they saw Carly, as if embarrassed by what she had caught them doing in the woods. Carly wanted to tell them it wasn't their fault, but how could she explain about the griddlebeast? Several people even looked angrily at her.

When the bell rang for the study period, Carly was the first one out the classroom door. In the library, she made sure no one was watching and went quickly to the dark aisle where the chimney to the cabin was. She slid the books to the side and climbed down the ladder. At the bottom, she knocked on the wood wall; Green was waiting for her.

Climbing out of the fireplace, Carly saw that Elzick was again standing on top of the Crank. "Is your grandmother back?" she asked.

"Not yet," said Green.

They were both getting worried.

They hadn't seen Granny Pitcher since the night the whistle root trees rang. Green hadn't gone to school because he wanted to be at the cabin when she came back.

But he had just finished making them both some hot tea when the front door swung open.

"Hello, hello," called Granny Pitcher, marching in from the tunnel. "Did you make enough tea for three?" She shook off her ragged cloak and sat down at the table with them.

"Where have you been?" asked Green, getting up to pour a third mug of tea. His tone was brusque, but Carly could tell how relieved he was to see her.

"On a bit of a hunt," said Granny Pitcher. She patted his hand when he handed her the mug and smiled at him. "I'm sorry I worried you. I didn't plan to be gone so long."

"On a hunt for what?"

"Oh, the griddlebeast . . ." Granny Pitcher closed her eyes and drank her tea; her strong hands seemed to savor the warmth from the chipped old mug.

"Is it still out there?" asked Carly. Had the whistle root trees failed? Were they all still in danger? Green dropped into the chair beside her with a worried look on his face.

Granny Pitcher swallowed her tea and opened her eyes. "It is still out there . . . but the whistle root trees have done their magic well, children. We don't need to worry about its whispers anymore."

"Did they change the griddlebeast into a tree?" asked Green. "Like they did to the kings in the End-root?"

Granny Pitcher smiled. "The whistle root trees don't always . . . well, you can't predict what they're going to do when you turn the Crank. Now, let me tell you what I did find. It took much searching, but I eventually came across a little bird of a kind I'd never seen before. It was only slightly bigger than a sparrow, but had something of the look of an owl, mainly

"Now, let me tell you what I did find."

about the feathers. It seemed enormously proud of those feathers, and spent most of its time admiring their reflection in the creek. Every now and then it would try to chase a rabbit, although it was too small to do much more than startle them or tug an ear. I followed it for quite some time. It never sang or made a sound. I don't think it has a voice. I have decided to call it a griddlebird. The name seems an obvious choice, wouldn't you agree?"

Carly and Green both sat still, then nodded and grinned, marveling at the griddlebeast's fate and the power of the whistle root trees.

"Yes, but..." Carly began, and then stopped, thinking about exactly what she wanted to ask. "Granny Pitcher, why was there a griddlebeast at all?"

The old woman sipped her tea and studied them both solemnly. "Revenge, my dear," she said finally. "A griddlebeast is always an instrument of revenge. Though whoever uses a griddlebeast for that purpose must be patient, because you never know when it's going to hatch from its egg of stone. It could be days, or years, or ... centuries, as was the case with ours."

"The split rock!" said Carly. "That's what it hatched

from, isn't it? I found it in the woods. And one of the messages from the Woop said to beware of broken rocks. He was trying to warn us!"

"Yes," said Granny Pitcher, narrowing her eyes and reminding Carly of the fierce woman she'd seen in the newspaper picture. "Though he could have been a little more direct with his warning, couldn't he? And it wasn't very kind to leave you in the griddlebeast's burrow. But I suppose we must thank him for sending you the wind. He did do that . . . at least."

"But where did the rock come from?" asked Green.

"From the Endroot," said Granny Pitcher. "From the Moon King's oldest brother. For you see, after he chopped down the whistle root trees, and after the Moon King left with the rats, he foolishly allowed all the other trees to be chopped down as well. And once they were gone, the Endroot quickly returned to the wasteland of ashes it had been before.

"The constant winds and swirling ash drove the oldest brother mad. And as the years passed and his madness deepened, he began to believe that the Moon King had cursed his kingdom as punishment for what had been done to him — even though the destruction of the Endroot had been entirely the oldest brother's own fault.

"So he sent a gallowhawk — the same kind of bird that dropped Crassifolia into the Endroot — to find the Moon King. And after several months of flying over mountains, oceans, and deserts, the gallowhawk did find him, here, and dropped the rock from which the griddlebeast would one day hatch — although I'm sure the oldest brother hoped it would hatch much sooner than it did. He intended to punish the Moon King, you see, and everything connected to him — the rats, the whistle root trees, and, as it turned out, his family, for the Moon King had married a young woman who bravely entered the woods that everyone else thought were haunted. A few of their descendants are still living, but most have moved away."

Granny Pitcher paused, sipped her tea, and smiled. "And none of them know their history. Although two of them have learned it . . . today. I should probably have told them sooner, but I feared they would think me nothing more than a crazy old woman with a head full of foolish stories."

There was silence in the cabin. Carly and Green looked at her in shock.

"You mean us?" said Green. "Carly and me?"

"Yes . . . you are descended from the Moon King through your mother, Green, and Carly through her father. He certainly got the family genes, didn't he? Traveling and playing music — that goes right back to the earliest days in the Endroot. And you, Carly, inherited the Moon King's most distinguishing trait of all, though I know it has made life hard for you. I had assumed your aunt was taking good care of you . . ."

Carly looked down. Granny Pitcher reached over and gently lifted Carly's chin with her hand. "But now I see that I was wrong. Please forgive me, dear child. I should have made you part of our little family long before now."

Carly smiled and felt the blurry beginning of tears. Her head, however, was spinning with questions. "But how do you know all this?" she asked.

Granny Pitcher didn't answer right away, and gazed at Carly thoughtfully with her ancient amber eyes. She started to say something but stopped, looked at Green lovingly, and said instead, "Why, the stories, of course, my dear. I thought they were lost when they took the cabin from me. I didn't leave peacefully, you know — when they built the school — and I was only able to grab a couple of things before they dragged me out the door. Then Green found the first story and I realized that they still existed — in the library of all places, right above our heads, though we still have several more to find. But for now, I have something else to show you."

Granny Pitcher stood up and went to one of the windows. She opened the locked shutters with a key from around her neck. A space had been dug where the window should have been. She pulled out a wooden case and walked back to the table. "Go ahead and open it," she said.

Carly and Green flipped a few stiff latches and opened the dusty lid. They both gasped when they saw a very old fiddle inside with a small crescent moon delicately carved in it.

"Is it . . . did it belong to . . ." Carly tried to ask.

"It was the Moon King's," said Granny Pitcher. "And it was his father's before him. But it was traveling with their family in the Endroot long before even that. Oh, and let's see now . . ."

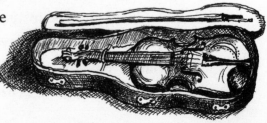

Granny Pitcher walked back to the open window. "Too many whistle root trees were lost this week. But luckily, I was able to grab one other thing when I was taken from the cabin." She reached past the shutters, pulled something out, and walked back toward them. "I'm giving it to both of you, along with the fiddle. I think you'll know what to do ..."

Carly watched in disbelief, despite everything that had happened, as Granny Pitcher dropped a small bag on the table between her and Green.

Without even looking inside, Carly knew it contained seeds.

"TEACH YOU TO PLAY the fiddle?" said Lewis irritably several nights later in the rats' cave.

"And Green too," Carly reminded him.

"What? The boy who sleeps in tunnels?"

"I thought we could listen when you start teaching the new musicians, now that the owls are dancing again. We'll even bring our own fiddle."

"I should think you'll have to," said Lewis, looking critically at the size of her fingers.

Small flames burned festively throughout the village, one atop every house. The rats had returned and made their chimneys into candlesticks, stuffing them with bits of wick and wax.

"I never would have told the other rats everything that happened if I knew they were going to make this fuss," said Lewis. "Moon Queen . . . who ever heard of such nonsense? You're a musician, and there's no greater honor than that."

"I know," said Carly, smiling at him. She was wearing the crown of twigs, ivy, and flowers that Breeza Meezy had given her during the ceremony, which had been a complete surprise when she arrived at the cave earlier. She was also sitting in the Moon King's chair.

Carly stood suddenly and ran toward the entrance to the cave. She went straight to the old whistle root tree.

Standing at its feet, she held her breath and tapped it sharply.

It didn't shimmer, and the Moon Queen of Whistle Root happily returned to her throne.

The END